F/

THE HOUSE ON THE BORDERLAND

The House on the Borderland

*From the Manuscript, discovered in 1877 by
Messrs. Tonnison and Berreggnog, in the
Ruins that lie to the South of the
Village of Kraighten, in the West
of Ireland. Set out here,
with Notes*

by

William Hope Hodgson

The Swan River Press
Dublin, Ireland
MMXVIII

The House on the Borderland
by William Hope Hodgson

Published by
The Swan River Press
Dublin, Ireland
in Late April, MMXVIII

www.swanriverpress.ie
brian@swanriverpress.ie

Introduction © Alan Moore
Illustrations © John Coulthart
Afterword © Iain Sinclair
This Edition © Swan River Press

Dust jacket and cover design by Meggan Kehrli
from artwork by John Coulthart.

Set in Garamond by Ken Mackenzie

ISBN 978-1-78380-021-6

The House on the Borderland
is limited to 350 copies.

Contents

Fear of a Porous Border:
William Hope Hodgson's
Liminal Masterpiece

While there are, admittedly, more than a few duplications in the arrested avalanche of books that I prefer to think of as my library, the volume that I seem to have deliberately acquired the most editions of is, by a long chalk, W. H. Hodgson's endlessly intriguing *The House on the Borderland.* Why that should be I'm not entirely certain, and can only put it down to the peculiar sense of aura that surrounds the author's eerie and majestic work, particularly this penultimate and most unsettling vision. Almost from the moment that you hear the title—personally, this was while absorbing H. P. Lovecraft's essay "Supernatural Horror in Literature", a probable point of entry for most readers of that period—you are infected by the novel's weird charisma, although possibly not to the point of spending the next fifty years obsessively accruing different versions of the same text.

The first acquisition, picked up as a fifteen year-old schoolboy in the heady summer drift of 1969, was that year's Panther paperback reissue, the first time that Hodgson's tour de force had been in print in England since 1921, rebranded by its trippy Alan Aldridge packaging as a precursor to late-Sixties psychedelia: a bright pink title in a children's-book font set against metallic silver, with accompanying cover-doodle of an indigo brick edifice shaped like a screaming skull and thronged by crappy cartoon ghosts; a poorly thought-through *Grand Designs* conversion, its relationship to Hodgson's story somewhere between tenuous and non-existent. Although, in all fairness, what could anybody reasonably expect from something retailing at less than twenty pence in the new money?

Later purchases, it must be said, while more expensive, came no closer in their cover illustrations to conveying any real sense of what *The House on the Borderland* concealed beneath its boards. Published in 1946, the Arkham House edition—with its dust jacket a lurid chimera-menagerie that seems to be engaged in kettling the pencil elevation of a relatively modern house, by the more usually brilliant Hannes Bok—also avoids direct engagement with the novel's radioactive content, as does the much later Grafton paperback, adorned with visuals more suitable to a mid-Seventies collection from Clark Ashton Smith, and picked up solely for the laser-focus afterword by Iain Sinclair, which you are fortunate enough to find included in this current volume. In fact, prior to the equally-discerning landing of John Coulthart to provide this new edition's wraps and illustrations, one could be readily excused for the assumption that previous artists were acquainted with the work through no more than an inside-flap synopsis, and that the sole brush or stylus capable of reproducing Hodgson's imagery was that of Hodgson's luminescent prose itself.

This would appear to be the strategy behind my own copy of the 1908 Chapman and Hall first, an all but unique treasure, beautifully rebound with its gold-lettered emerald boards replaced, as with the endpapers, by an hallucinatory seethe of marbling. Other than photographs of Hodgson's home "Glaneifion" in Borth on the Welsh coast included by Nick Austin, the tome's thoughtful and fastidious former owner, there are no attempts to illustrate the revelations of the narrative, neither tipped-in Willy Pogany colour plates nor even Sidney Sime monochrome chapter-headings such as might be found within a Blackwood or a Machen product of the day. Perhaps fantastical embellishments were consciously avoided, so as not to undermine the carefully-contrived "found footage" aspect of the tale by flagging up its mind-bending deliriums, or perhaps its publishers considered Hodgson's book to be an oddball long-shot and unlikely to recoup even without the cost involved in finding a delineator. Given the flat absence of public reaction to *House on the Borderland*'s first publication, despite favourable reviews, and the similarly blank response to a second edition some thirteen years later, this last motive would have been entirely justified: the firework that had promised such a staggering celestial display had failed to go off in the early-twentieth century's damp and shell-pocked mud; would need almost another fifty years before achieving even limited and sputtering ignition.

During that same period, in those lost aeons, Hodgson's fellow chroniclers of the fantastic—Machen, Blackwood, Lovecraft and Dunsany—had attained cult status and were taken seriously by a gradually expanding circle of admirers. This raises the question as to why what happened in the case of Lovecraft's Arkham or Lord Dunsany's Pegāna didn't take place when it came to Hodgson's Borderland. Was its potential audience alienated by the lack of a conventional weird story format with a final-chapter revelation/explanation/exorcism of the book's uncanny element? After all, in Hodgson's book plot is replaced by a fluorescent seizure, a bone-rattling fugue state, and when this is at last spent the novel ends. Did buyers keep away, as with the equally-neglected David Lindsay's dazzling *A Voyage to Arcturus*, because they found its universe-annihilating visionary rush inscrutable or, otherwise, because of its alarming resonance? In short, did the prospective readership avoid the work because they couldn't understand it, or because they feared they might?

Before attempting to resolve this point in an examination of the text, perhaps a few words on its little-known creator are required. Born on November 15th, 1877, to the sprawling family of an impoverished Essex clergyman, the strikingly good-looking fourteen year-old Hodgson flew the cramped and over-intimate domestic coop by hurriedly running away to sea in 1891, his father Samuel Hodgson dying of throat cancer shortly afterwards. That this storm-tossed and lurching interval would provide inspiration for the tales of supernatural maritime encounters, like *The Boats of the Glen Carrig*, that make up the greater part of Hodgson's fiction, is unquestionable. As to what this period's emotional and personal impact upon the author might have been, however, we are left to draw whatever inference we can from the fact that, on once more making landfall and commencing properly his literary career, Hodgson's first published writings were instruction books on body building, physical development, and self-defence. It may be that out on the ocean waves, an element that he would ever after feel a great antipathy towards, he had encountered men at their most swinish.

Back on dry ground, living with his widowed mother in impoverishment at their three-storey seafront home in Borth, it was a memory of one of the family's many relocations as they followed cleric Samuel Hodgson from parish to parish, on this particular occasion settling in County Galway on the western coast of Ireland, that provided the titular edifice of his most famous work, perching uneasily astride its cliff-top chasm. It may be that there's some evidence here to suggest a different reading of the term psychogeography, an implication that some places might be haunted by the future fictions that they will one day inspire, as if specific narratives were already embedded in specific landscapes, a variety of unexploded dream-bomb: Iain Sinclair cites a visit to the same spot a few decades later by the author Iris Murdoch, herself captivated by the same precarious dwelling and, without prior knowledge of *House on the Borderland* or Hodgson, seemingly compelled to write the eerie building as inhabited by a haunted recluse in her book *The Unicorn*. Language, event, and character, curled foetal in the fissured rock.

After what must have been the disappointment of his book's subdued reception, Hodgson would return to his more customary seafaring supernaturalism in his novel *The Ghost Pirates*, published in 1909, and then would pen one final work of sweeping vision with his monumental and syntactically unusual, faux-archaic tale of epic love in a perpetually nocturnal world-to-come, *The Night Land*, published by Eveleigh Nash in 1912. The author at this point would have been only thirty-five, recently married to agony-column writer Betty Farnworth, and it's both painful and tantalising to imagine the invention and the scale of any subsequent cosmic excursions that he may have been considering had it not been for the First World War's outbreak two years later. Or perhaps the lack of a discernible reaction to his most accomplished works had served a bromide to that quadrant of his literary enthusiasm, and it's possible he knew that there was no grand and mysterious next project like a lover yet to be encountered, waiting just a little further down the road. He was still writing: a stripped-down 10,000-word reworking of *The Night Land* and a number of short stories in commercial genres, but the soaring pinnacle of his originality and his unique imagination was behind him now. Hodgson's enlistment may have been choosing a literal no-man's land over that of the empty page. Certainly, when he was recipient of a much-sought-after non-fatal wound, head injuries and a broken jaw, that would allow a man now forty years old to retire with honour from the battlefield, Hodgson's dogged insistence on returning to the fray and suffering a non-non-fatal wound from a direct hit by a shell in the war's final months is not suggestive of somebody with a new and stupefying metaphysical quartet in mind. I don't mean to suggest that the author was suicidal, or indeed that he was anything but an exceptionally brave and honourable Edwardian man with a desire to serve his country; simply that he may have known his most important works would never in his lifetime bring him recognition, and an ending in a literal if not a literary blaze of glory at the Fourth Battle of Ypres may have appeared to be the preferable option.

This leaves nothing save his twilight travelogue itself as a surviving witness open to interrogation, even if we're given the impression that its testimony is concealing something. Starting with the title page's claim to the work's derivation—"From the Manuscript, discovered in 1877 by Messrs. Tonnison and Berreggnog, in the Ruins that lie to the south of the Village of Kraighten, in the West of Ireland. Set out here, with notes"—continuing through Hodgson's "Introduction to the Manuscript" where he purports to be its disconcerted editor, the reader finds herself engaging with a set of nested contexts that presumably are there to lend a sense of documentary verisimilitude to the delirious account: the curiously-named hiking companions have unearthed a partly damaged journal from amidst sinister ruins and, bewildered by its content, have then for some reason passed it on to little-known purveyor of marine ghost-stories W. H. Hodgson who, in turn, presents it with some trepidation to his publishers and thence his readership. Fantasy authors of that era, treading water in the glittering black wake of Edgar Allan Poe, would not infrequently confect elaborate accounts of how reality-defying narratives had come to reach their audience, establishing fictitious paper-trails and referencing non-existent scholarship in an attempt to smudge the boundary between the fluid world in which their tale occurs and the adjacent, far more concrete world where it is being read in a well-lit contemporary living room. The tactic in itself is not unusual, although in *The House on the Borderland* there is a sense that the contextualising brackets of Tonnison and Berreggnog's diary notes or Hodgson's "editorial" introduction are included not so much to lend the work a spurious credibility as to provide a double-sheath of prophylactic layers between its infectious content and its public. One is left with a suspicion that contained within this flimsy shielding there is at the novel's fissile core some heavy element, experiential or emotional, that is too personal and radioactive for its author to approach with safety.

As to what this element might be, perhaps a clue rests in the novel's dedication, "To My Father (Whose feet tread the lost aeons)", with this followed by an urgent, cosmically accented poem on mortality that is attributed to something called *Shoon of the Dead*, as if this latter were a well-known work of classical or biblical antiquity, "shoon" being an archaic dialect rendering of "shoes". With Samuel Hodgson's death coming so soon upon the heels of his son running off to sea, it's difficult not to suspect some residue of guilt left as a tide-mark on the prodigal's self-image, an impression reinforced by the inclusion of a second poem, "Grief", a distraught meditation on bereavement that's positioned after Hodgson's pseudo-editorial "Introduction to the Manuscript", having a footnote by the supposed editor declaring that the poem was discovered pencilled on a sheet of foolscap, gummed behind the flyleaf of the journal unearthed by Tonnison and Berreggnog on their camping expedition to the West of Ireland. This, presumably, is meant to indicate that the stanzas of "Grief" ("They have all the appearance of having been written at an earlier date than the Manuscript") are actually the work of the Recluse who is the tale's narrator, yet the similarity to "To My Father" in both tone and content only serves to further minimise the distance between Hodgson and his psychologically assaulted character.

It is then possible that Hodgson's sense of being truant in his filial duties—off at sea, apprenticed as a cabin boy instead of being at his father's deathbed—helped provide an impetus for the creation of *House on the Borderland*'s jaw-dropping eschatology, though it seems likely that the truancy was at least partially ideological: considering that Hodgson was the eldest or the second-eldest son of an Anglican minister, his vision of the cosmos as presented here and in *The Night Land* would seem to be that of a markedly Godless universe. For all of the devotion evident in "To My Father" and the desolated loss of "Grief", it could well be that the relationship was a conflicted one upon some basic theological and existential level. After all, when we recall his vehement aversion to the sea (despite qualifications as a sailor, with war's outbreak he enlisted with the army rather than the navy), it appears more probable that Hodgson's nautical adventures as a fourteen year-old represented not so much movement towards some longed-for dream career as a movement away from the familial situation he was anxious to escape. That the boy's father may have nurtured aspirations that his son would follow him into the clergy is perhaps implied by that unusual middle name.

But even if the turbulent emotions that surround a parent's death provided the initial formless urge to write a novel, they do not sufficiently explain the book that Hodgson came to write, or how a personal emotional calamity could be scaled up until it finally became the end of everything.

The book defies any such biographical interpretation from its opening fugue, the ten-mile-wide arena ringed by either mountains carved into the forms of ancient gods or else colossal deities that have been petrified, where at the centre, menaced by a porcine monster that is its equivalent in size, there stands a green jade reconstruction of the stunned narrator's residence—all this in the first dozen or so pages of the central manuscript. By novel's end, of course, with planets screaming as they fall into the prescient abyss of a "black sun", there would seem no remaining possibility that Hodgson's pyrotechnic Armageddon stood for anything as relatively commonplace as a paternal loss.

And yet throughout the endlessly imploding cosmic vistas there endures the notion that this universal cataclysm is at the same time a world's end visited upon a single individual, possibly the Recluse, or Hodgson, or the reader. Certainly, some kind of identification seems apparent in Hodgson's decision to have his two travellers chance upon the buried journal in 1877, this being the year of Hodgson's birth, which, given the plot difficulties that it introduces—why did the alarmed Tonnison and Berreggnog wait for thirty years before forwarding their mysterious tome to Hodgson?—seems to indicate the date can only have been chosen for its personal association. Though its ratios are landscape, it's hard not to feel that this book is intended as internal portrait; that, as Iain Sinclair's afterword and Alan Aldridge's bad-trip embellishments suggest, the house is, in the last analysis, a human skull that does not differentiate between the universe of the astronomers and that of its perceptions, does not separate the outside from the inside; where the end of either is the end of all. A reader picking up the book expecting to resort to the harmless imaginary will instead discover she is lost in the symbolic, that mode of address that ushers us, by stealth, uncomfortably closer to the real.

Upon consideration, is it this refusal to distinguish between personal and pan-galactic that simultaneously lends *House on the Borderland* its shadowy charisma and erects the reputational electric force-field which, historically, seems to deter the buying public? With its containing intermediary narratives—Tonnison and Berreggnog; Hodgson—only adding to the ambiguity surrounding what this book is actually saying and who's saying it, is it the paradoxical absence of well-marked boundaries or borders that supplies the novel's jolt of non-specific dread, its charge that either attracts or repels? The lack of a conventional conclusion, as remarked on earlier, is similarly working to remove one of the main protective barriers between the writing and its audience, the point of literal closure where the narrative's enigmas are resolved and we can shut a cardboard back door sprayed with its graffiti of critically favourable quotations, sealing the continuum of the story off from the continuum in which we are, and think, and live. No such securing of the premises is possible with Hodgson's book, permitting its contained reality to leak, potentially to bleed into the reader's own. Houses on borders, it should be remembered, are at once marking a boundary and breaching it.

Is the fragility of boundaries ultimately what the book's about? The apprehension that our relatively comfortable existence is a delicate soap-bubble of a thing suspended in a largely unimaginable and chaotic universe, when at any moment there might come some unexpected interruption—the death of a patriarch; the Archduke's limo inexplicably pulled to a halt outside a Sarajevo coffee house; a rendezvous with an artillery shell; the unanticipated outcome of a referendum or election—puncturing reality and letting all the pig-beasts up from underneath the floorboards of the world where, in our hearts, we knew that they were hiding all along?

In Iain Sinclair's startling novel *Radon Daughters*, 1994 (and no, obviously, that's not included here but makes an unsurpassable companion to the present volume, and I'd recommend you find yourself a copy of it as soon as is possible), the central character has been employed to seek out and secure a rumoured sequel to *House on the Borderland* for his sinister government employers, as if there could be a sequel to a book that ends the universe. The reason for the secret state's anxiety regarding this obscure, almost forgotten fantasy is based upon the fear that, should such an unlikely sequel reawaken public interest in Hodgson's greatest work, the borderland could become a universal condition. Given the distressed state of our current century—teetering on its crag above an economic, social and environmental chasm, worried by the increasingly voluble subhuman grunting from its cellar—Sinclair's diagnosis seems a lot less fanciful than it may have appeared on its initial twentieth-century publication. It is this un-quarantined, infectious quality that we intuit in Hodgson's literary crescendo that explains our fascination, nearly justifies those multiple editions, and excuses the book's absent readership that turned back at the House's doorstep in their droves.

In these new times, with this extremely reverent new edition, let us hope that this extraordinary book of revelations can at last emerge into a landscape complex and extreme enough to recognise Hodgson's incendiary magnum opus as a unique mapping of contemporary psychology; as an invaluable cartography of the new land, the future that we refugees from the fragmented present teem towards for sanctuary, for respite from the strobing aeons. Knock and enter at your own liability.

Alan Moore
Northampton
February 20, 2017

The House on the Borderland

To My Father
(Whose feet tread the lost aeons)

"Open the door,
　　And listen!
Only the wind's muffled roar,
　　And the glisten
Of tears round the moon.
　　And, in fancy, the tread
Of vanishing shoon—
　　Out in the night with the Dead.

"Hush! And hark
　　To the sorrowful cry
Of the wind in the dark.
　　Hush and hark, without murmur or sigh,
　　　To shoon that tread the lost aeons:
　　To the sound that bids you to die.
Hush and hark! Hush and Hark!"

Shoon of the Dead

Introduction to the Manuscript

Many are the hours in which I have pondered upon the story that is set forth in the following pages. I trust that my instincts are not awry when they prompt me to leave the account, in simplicity, as it was handed to me.

And the MS. itself—You must picture me, when first it was given into my care, turning it over, curiously, and making a swift, jerky examination. A small book it is; but thick, and all, save the last few pages, filled with a quaint but legible handwriting, and writ very close. I have the queer, faint, pit-water smell of it in my nostrils now as I write, and my fingers have subconscious memories of the soft, "cloggy" feel of the long-damp pages.

I recall, with just a slight effort, my first impression of the worded contents of the book—an impression of the fantastic, gathered from casual glances, and an unconcentrated attention.

Then, conceive of me comfortably a-seat for the evening, and the little, squat book and I, companions for some close, solitary hours. And the change that came upon my judgement! The emergence of a half-belief. From a *seeming* "fantasia" there grew, to reward my unbiased concentration, a cogent, coherent scheme of ideas that gripped my interest more securely than the mere bones of the *account* or *story*, whichever it be, and I confess to an inclination to use the first term. I found a greater story within the lesser—and the paradox is no paradox.

5

I read, and, in reading, lifted the Curtains of the Impossible that blind the mind, and looked out into the unknown. Amid stiff, abrupt sentences I wandered; and, presently, I had no fault to charge against their abrupt tellings; for, better far than my own ambitious phrasing, is this mutilated story capable of bringing home all that the old Recluse, of the vanished house, had striven to tell.

Of the simple, stiffly given account of weird and extraordinary matters, I will say little. It lies before you. The inner story must be uncovered, personally, by each reader, according to ability and desire. And even should any fail to see, as now I see, the shadowed picture and conception of that to which one may well give the accepted titles of Heaven and Hell; yet can I promise certain thrills, merely taking the story as a story.

One final impression, and I will cease from troubling. I cannot but look upon the account of the Celestial Globes as a striking illustration (how nearly had I said "proof"!) of the actuality of our thoughts and emotions among the Realities. For, without seeming to suggest the annihilation of the lasting reality of Matter, as the hub and framework of the Machine of Eternity, it enlightens one with conceptions of the existence of worlds of thought and emotion, working in conjunction with, and duly subject to, the scheme of material creation.

William Hope Hodgson
"Glaneifion"
Borth, Cardiganshire
December 17, 1907

Grief *

"Fierce hunger reigns within my breast,
    I had not dreamt that this whole world,
        Crushed in the hand of God, could yield
Such bitter essence of unrest,
    Such pain as Sorrow now hath hurled
        Out of its dreadful heart, unsealed!

"Each sobbing breath is but a cry,
    My heart-strokes knells of agony,
        And my whole brain has but one thought
That nevermore through life shall I
    (Save in the ache of memory)
        Touch hands with thee, who now art naught!

"Through the whole void of night I search,
    So dumbly crying out to thee;
        But thou are *not*; and night's vast throne
Becomes an all stupendous church
    With star-bells knelling unto me
        Who in all space am most alone!

"An hungered, to the shore I creep,
    Perchance some comfort waits on me
        From the old Sea's eternal heart;
But lo! from all the solemn deep,
    Far voices out of mystery
        Seem questioning why we are apart!

Grief

"Where'er I go I am alone
    Who once, through thee, had all the world.
      My breast is one whole raging pain
For that which *was*, and now is flown
    Into the Blank where life is hurled
      Where all is not, nor is again!

* These stanzas I found, in pencil, upon a piece of foolscap gummed in behind the fly-leaf of the MS. They have all the appearance of having been written at an earlier date than the Manuscript.—Ed.

Chapter I
The Finding of the Manuscript

Right away in the west of Ireland lies a tiny hamlet called Kraighten. It is situated, alone, at the base of a low hill. Far around there spreads a waste of bleak and totally inhospitable country; where, here and there at great intervals, one may come upon the ruins of some long desolate cottage—unthatched and stark. The whole land is bare and unpeopled, the very earth scarcely covering the rock that lies beneath it, and with which the country abounds, in places rising out of the soil in wave-shaped ridges.

Yet, in spite of its desolation, my friend Tonnison and I had elected to spend our vacation there. He had stumbled on the place by mere chance the year previously, during the course of a long walking tour, and discovered the possibilities for the angler in a small and unnamed river that runs past the outskirts of the little village.

I have said that the river is without name; I may add that no map that I have hitherto consulted has shown either village or stream. They seem to have entirely escaped observation: indeed, they might never exist for all that the average guide tells one. Possibly this can be partly accounted for by the fact that the nearest railway station (Ardrahan) is some forty miles distant.

It was early one warm evening when my friend and I arrived in Kraighten. We had reached Ardrahan the previous night, sleeping there in rooms hired at the village post office, and leaving in good time on the following morning, clinging insecurely to one of the typical jaunting cars.

It had taken us all day to accomplish our journey over some of the roughest tracks imaginable, with the result that we were thoroughly tired and somewhat bad tempered. However, the tent had to be erected and our goods stowed away before we could think of food or rest. And so we set to work, with the aid of our driver, and soon had the tent up upon a small patch of ground just outside the little village, and quite near to the river.

Then, having stored all our belongings, we dismissed the driver, as he had to make his way back as speedily as possible, and told him to come across to us at the end of a fortnight. We had brought sufficient provisions to last us for that space of time, and water we could get from the stream. Fuel we did not need, as we had included a small oil-stove among our outfit, and the weather was fine and warm.

It was Tonnison's idea to camp out instead of getting lodgings in one of the cottages. As he put it, there was no joke in sleeping in a room with a numerous family of healthy Irish in one corner and the pigsty in the other, while overhead a ragged colony of roosting fowls distributed their blessings impartially, and the whole place so full of peat smoke that it made a fellow sneeze his head off just to put it inside the doorway.

Tonnison had got the stove lit now and was busy cutting slices of bacon into the frying pan; so I took the kettle and walked down to the river for water. On the way, I had to pass close to a little group of the village people, who eyed me curiously, but not in any unfriendly manner, though none of them ventured a word.

As I returned with my kettle filled, I went up to them and, after a friendly nod, to which they replied in like manner, I asked them casually about the fishing; but, instead of answering, they just shook their heads silently, and stared at me. I repeated the question, addressing more particularly a great, gaunt fellow at my elbow; yet again I received no answer. Then the man turned to a comrade and said something rapidly in a language that I did not understand; and, at once, the whole crowd of them fell to jabbering in what, after a few moments, I guessed to be pure Irish. At the same time they cast many glances in my direction. For a minute, perhaps, they spoke among themselves thus; then the man I had addressed faced round at me and said something. By the expression of his face I guessed that he, in turn, was questioning me; but now I had to shake my head, and indicate that I did not comprehend what it was they wanted to know; and so we stood looking at one another, until I heard Tonnison calling to me to hurry up with the kettle. Then, with a smile and a nod, I left them, and all in the little crowd smiled and nodded in return, though their faces still betrayed their puzzlement.

It was evident, I reflected as I went towards the tent, that the inhabitants of these few huts in the wilderness did not know a word of English; and when I told Tonnison, he remarked that he was aware of the fact, and, more, that it was not at all uncommon in that part of the country, where the people often lived and died in their isolated hamlets without ever coming in contact with the outside world.

"I wish we had got the driver to interpret for us before he left," I remarked, as we sat down to our meal. "It seems so strange for the people of this place not even to know what we've come for."

Tonnison grunted an assent, and thereafter was silent for a while.

Later, having satisfied our appetites somewhat, we began to talk, laying our plans for the morrow; then, after a smoke, we closed the flap of the tent, and prepared to turn in.

"I suppose there's no chance of those fellows outside taking anything?" I asked, as we rolled ourselves in our blankets.

Tonnison said that he did not think so, at least while we were about; and, as he went on to explain, we could lock up everything, except the tent, in the big chest that we had brought to hold our provisions. I agreed to this, and soon we were both asleep.

Next morning, early, we rose and went for a swim in the river; after which we dressed and had breakfast. Then we roused out our fishing tackle and overhauled it, by which time, our breakfasts having settled somewhat, we made all secure within the tent and strode off in the direction my friend had explored on his previous visit.

During the day we fished happily, working steadily up-stream, and by evening we had one of the prettiest creels of fish that I had seen for a long while. Returning to the village, we made a good feed off our day's spoil, after which, having selected a few of the finer fish for our breakfast, we presented the remainder to the group of villagers who had assembled at a respectful distance to watch our doings. They seemed wonderfully grateful, and heaped mountains of what I presumed to be Irish blessings upon our heads.

Thus we spent several days, having splendid sport, and first-rate appetites to do justice upon our prey. We were pleased to find how friendly the villagers were inclined to be, and that there was no evidence of their having ventured to meddle with our belongings during our absences.

It was on a Tuesday that we arrived in Kraighten, and it would be on the Sunday following that we made a great discovery. Hitherto we had always gone up-stream; on that day, however, we laid aside our rods, and, taking some provisions, set off for a long ramble in the opposite direction. The day was warm, and we trudged along leisurely enough, stopping about mid-day to eat our lunch upon a great flat rock near the riverbank. Afterwards, we sat and smoked awhile, resuming our walk only when we were tired of inaction.

For perhaps another hour we wandered onward, chatting quietly and comfortably on this and that matter, and on several occasions stopping while my companion—who is something of an artist—made rough sketches of striking bits of the wild scenery.

And then, without any warning whatsoever, the river we had followed so confidently, came to an abrupt end—vanishing into the earth.

"Good Lord!" I said, "who ever would have thought of this?"

And I stared in amazement; then I turned to Tonnison. He was looking, with a blank expression upon his face, at the place where the river disappeared.

In a moment he spoke.

"Let us go on a bit; it may reappear again—anyhow, it is worth investigating."

I agreed, and we went forward once more, though rather aimlessly; for we were not at all certain in which direction to prosecute our search. For perhaps a mile we moved onward; then Tonnison, who had been gazing about curiously, stopped and shaded his eyes.

"See!" he said, after a moment, "isn't that mist or something, over there to the right—away in a line with that great piece of rock?" And he indicated with his hand.

I stared, and, after a minute, seemed to see something, but could not be certain, and said so.

"Anyway," my friend replied, "we'll just go across and have a glance." And he started off in the direction he had suggested, I following. Presently, we came among bushes, and, after a time, out upon the top of a high, boulder-strewn bank, from which we looked down into a wilderness of bushes and trees.

"Seems as though we had come upon an oasis in this desert of stone," muttered Tonnison, as he gazed interestedly. Then he was silent, his eyes fixed; and I looked also; for up from somewhere about the centre of the wooded lowland there rose high into the quiet air a great column of haze-like spray, upon which the sun shone, causing innumerable rainbows.

"How beautiful!" I exclaimed.

"Yes," answered Tonnison, thoughtfully. "There must be a waterfall, or something, over there. Perhaps it's our river come to light again. Let's go and see."

Down the sloping bank we made our way, and entered among the trees and shrubberies. The bushes were matted, and the trees overhung us, so that the place was disagreeably gloomy; though not dark enough to hide from me the fact that many of the trees were fruit trees, and that, here and there, one could trace indistinctly, signs of a long departed cultivation. Thus it came to me that we were making our way through the riot of a great and ancient garden. I said as much to Tonnison, and he agreed that there certainly seemed reasonable grounds for my belief.

What a wild place it was, so dismal and sombre! Somehow, as we went forward, a sense of the silent loneliness and desertion of the old garden grew upon me, and I felt shivery. One could imagine things lurking among the tangled bushes; while, in the very air of the place, there seemed something uncanny. I think Tonnison was conscious of this also, though he said nothing.

Suddenly, we came to a halt. Through the trees there had grown upon our ears a distant sound. Tonnison bent forward, listening. I could hear it more plainly now; it was continuous and harsh—a sort of droning roar, seeming to come from far away. I experienced a queer, indescribable, little feeling of nervousness. What sort of place was it into which we had got? I looked at my companion, to see what he thought of the matter; and noted that there was only puzzlement in his face; and then, as I watched his features, an expression of comprehension crept over them, and he nodded his head.

"That's a waterfall," he exclaimed, with conviction. "I know the sound now." And he began to push vigorously through the bushes, in the direction of the noise.

As we went forward, the sound became plainer continually, showing that we were heading straight towards it. Steadily, the roaring grew louder and nearer, until it appeared, as I remarked to Tonnison, almost to come from under our feet—and still we were surrounded by the trees and shrubs.

"Take care!" Tonnison called to me. "Look where you're going." And then, suddenly, we came out from among the trees, on to a great open space, where, not six paces in front of us, yawned the mouth of a tremendous chasm, from the depths of which the noise appeared to rise, along with the continuous, mist-like spray that we had witnessed from the top of the distant bank.

For quite a minute we stood in silence, staring in bewilderment at the sight; then my friend went forward cautiously to the edge of the abyss. I followed, and, together, we looked down through a boil of spray at a monster cataract of frothing water that burst, spouting, from the side of the chasm, nearly a hundred feet below.

"Good Lord!" said Tonnison.

I was silent, and rather awed. The sight was so unexpectedly grand and eerie; though this latter quality came more upon me later.

Presently, I looked up and across to the further side of the chasm. There, I saw something towering up among the spray: it looked like a fragment of a great ruin, and I touched Tonnison on the shoulder. He glanced round, with a start, and I pointed towards the thing. His gaze followed my finger, and his eyes lighted up with a sudden flash of excitement, as the object came within his field of view.

"Come along," he shouted above the uproar. "We'll have a look at it. There's something queer about this place; I feel it in my bones." And he started off, round the edge of the crater-like abyss. As we neared this new thing, I saw that I had not been mistaken in my first impression. It was undoubtedly a portion of some ruined building; yet now I made out that it was not built upon the edge of the chasm itself, as I had at first supposed; but perched almost at the extreme end of a huge spur of rock that jutted out some fifty or sixty feet over the abyss. In fact, the jagged mass of ruin was literally suspended in mid-air.

Arriving opposite it, we walked out on to the projecting arm of rock, and I must confess to having felt an intolerable sense of terror as I looked down from that dizzy perch into the unknown depths below us—into the deeps from which there rose ever the thunder of the falling water and the shroud of rising spray.

Reaching the ruin, we clambered round it cautiously, and, on the further side, came upon a mass of fallen stones and rubble. The ruin itself seemed to me, as I proceeded now to examine it minutely, to be a portion of the outer wall of some prodigious structure, it was so thick and substantially built; yet what it was doing in such a position I could by no means conjecture. Where was the rest of the house, or castle, or whatever there had been?

I went back to the outer side of the wall, and thence to the edge of the chasm, leaving Tonnison rooting systematically among the heap of stones and rubbish on the outer side. Then I commenced to examine the surface of the ground, near the edge of the abyss, to see whether there were not left other remnants of the building to which the fragment of ruin evidently belonged. But though I scrutinised the earth with the greatest care, I could see no signs of anything to show that there had ever been a building erected on the spot, and I grew more puzzled than ever.

Then, I heard a cry from Tonnison; he was shouting my name, excitedly, and without delay I hurried along the rocky promontory to the ruin. I wondered whether he had hurt himself, and then the thought came, that perhaps he had found something.

I reached the crumbled wall and climbed round. There I found Tonnison standing within a small excavation that he had made among the *débris*: he was brushing the dirt from something that looked like a book, much crumpled and dilapidated; and opening his mouth, every second or two, to bellow my name. As soon as he saw that I had come, he handed his prize to me, telling me to put it into my satchel so as to protect it from the damp, while he continued his explorations. This I did, first, however, running the pages through my fingers, and noting that they were closely filled with neat, old-fashioned writing which was quite legible, save in one portion, where many of the pages were almost destroyed, being muddied and crumpled, as though the book had been doubled back at that part. This, I found out from Tonnison, was actually as he had discovered it, and the damage was due, probably, to the fall of masonry upon the opened part. Curiously enough, the book was fairly dry, which I attributed to its having been so securely buried among the ruins.

Having put the volume away safely, I turned-to and gave Tonnison a hand with his self-imposed task of excavating; yet, though we put in over an hour's hard work, turning over the whole of the up-heaped stones and rubbish, we came upon nothing more than some fragments of broken wood, that might have been parts of a desk or table; and so we gave up searching, and went back along the rock, once more to the safety of the land.

The next thing we did was to make a complete tour of the tremendous chasm, which we were able to observe was in the form of an almost perfect circle, save for where the ruin-crowned spur of rock jutted out, spoiling its symmetry.

The abyss was, as Tonnison put it, like nothing so much as a gigantic well or pit going sheer down into the bowels of the earth.

For some time longer, we continued to stare about us, and then, noticing that there was a clear space away to the north of the chasm, we bent our steps in that direction.

Here, distant from the mouth of the mighty pit by some hundreds of yards, we came upon a great lake of silent water—silent, that is, save in one place where there was a continuous bubbling and gurgling.

Now, being away from the noise of the spouting cataract, we were able to hear one another speak, without having to shout at the tops of our voices, and I asked Tonnison what he thought of the place—I told him that I didn't like it, and that the sooner we were out of it the better I should be pleased.

He nodded in reply, and glanced at the woods behind furtively. I asked him if he had seen or heard anything. He made no answer; but stood silent, as though listening, and I kept quiet also.

Suddenly, he spoke.

"Hark!" he said, sharply. I looked at him, and then away among the trees and bushes, holding my breath involuntarily. A minute came and went in strained silence; yet I could hear nothing, and I turned to Tonnison to say as much; and then, even as I opened my lips to speak, there came a strange wailing noise out of the wood on our left . . . . It appeared to float through the trees, and there was a rustle of stirring leaves, and then silence.

All at once, Tonnison spoke, and put his hand on my shoulder. "Let us get out of here," he said, and began to move slowly towards where the surrounding trees and bushes seemed thinnest. As I followed him, it came to me suddenly that the sun was low, and that there was a raw sense of chilliness in the air.

Tonnison said nothing further, but kept on steadily. We were among the trees now, and I glanced around, nervously; but saw nothing, save the quiet branches and trunks and the tangled bushes. Onward we went, and no sound broke the silence, except the occasional snapping of a twig under our feet, as we moved forward. Yet, in spite of the quietness, I had a horrible feeling that we were not alone; and I kept so close to Tonnison that twice I kicked his heels clumsily, though he said nothing. A minute, and then another, and we reached the confines of the wood coming out at last upon the bare rockiness of the countryside. Only then was I able to shake off the haunting dread that had followed me among the trees.

Once, as we moved away, there seemed to come again a distant sound of wailing, and I said to myself that it was the wind—yet the evening was breathless.

Presently, Tonnison began to talk.

"Look you," he said with decision, "I would not spend the night in *that* place for all the wealth that the world holds. There is something unholy—diabolical—about it. It came to me all in a moment, just after you spoke. It seemed to me that the woods were full of vile things—you know!"

"Yes," I answered, and looked back towards the place; but it was hidden from us by a rise in the ground.

"There's the book," I said, and I put my hand into the satchel.

"You've got it safely?" he questioned, with a sudden access of anxiety.

"Yes," I replied.

19

"Perhaps," he continued, "we shall learn something from it when we get back to the tent. We had better hurry, too; we're a long way off still, and I don't fancy, now, being caught out here in the dark."

It was two hours later when we reached the tent; and, without delay, we set to work to prepare a meal; for we had eaten nothing since our lunch at midday.

Supper over, we cleared the things out of the way, and lit our pipes. Then Tonnison asked me to get the manuscript out of my satchel. This I did, and then, as we could not both read from it at the same time, he suggested that I should read the thing out loud. "And mind," he cautioned, knowing my propensities, "don't go skipping half the book."

Yet, had he but known what it contained, he would have realised how needless such advice was, for once at least. And there seated in the opening of our little tent, I began the strange tale of "The House on the Borderland" (for such was the title of the MS.); this is told in the following pages.

Chapter II
The Plain of Silence

"I am an old man. I live here in this ancient house, surrounded by huge, unkempt gardens.

"The peasantry, who inhabit the wilderness beyond, say that I am mad. That is because I will have nothing to do with them. I live here alone with my old sister, who is also my housekeeper. We keep no servants—I hate them. I have one friend, a dog; yes, I would sooner have old Pepper than the rest of Creation together. He, at least, understands me—and has sense enough to leave me alone when I am in my dark moods.

"I have decided to start a kind of diary; it may enable me to record some of the thoughts and feelings that I cannot express to anyone; but, beyond this, I am anxious to make some record of the strange things that I have heard and seen, during many years of loneliness, in this weird old building.

"For a couple of centuries, this house has had a reputation, a bad one, and, until I bought it, for more than eighty years no one had lived here; consequently, I got the old place at a ridiculously low figure.

"I am not superstitious; but I have ceased to deny that things happen in this old house—things that I cannot explain; and, therefore, I must needs ease my mind, by writing down an account of them, to the best of my ability; though, should this, my diary, ever be read when I am gone, the readers will but shake their heads, and be the more convinced that I was mad.

"This house, how ancient it is! though its age strikes one less, perhaps, than the quaintness of its structure, which is curious and fantastic to the last degree. Little curved towers and pinnacles, with outlines suggestive of leaping flames, predominate; while the body of the building is in the form of a circle.

"I have heard that there is an old story, told amongst the country people, to the effect that the devil built the place. However, that is as may be. True or not, I neither know nor care, save as it may have helped to cheapen it, ere I came.

"I must have been here some ten years before I saw sufficient to warrant any belief in the stories, current in the neighbourhood, about this house. It is true that I had, on at least a dozen occasions, seen, vaguely, things that puzzled me, and, perhaps, had felt more than I had seen. Then, as the years passed, bringing age upon me, I became often aware of something unseen, yet unmistakably present, in the empty rooms and corridors. Still, it was, as I have said, many years before I saw any real manifestations of the so-called supernatural.

"It was not Halloween. If I were telling a story for amusement's sake, I should probably place it on that night of nights; but this is a true record of my own experiences, and I would not put pen to paper to amuse anyone. No. It was after midnight on the morning of the twenty-first day of January. I was sitting reading, as is often my custom, in my study. Pepper lay, sleeping, near my chair.

"Without warning, the flames of the two candles went low, and then shone with a ghastly green effulgence. I looked up, quickly, and as I did so, I saw the lights sink into a dull, ruddy tint; so that the room glowed with a strange, heavy, crimson twilight that gave the shadows behind the

chairs and tables a double depth of blackness; and wherever the light struck, it was as though luminous blood had been splashed over the room.

"Down on the floor, I heard a faint, frightened whimper, and something pressed itself in between my two feet. It was Pepper, cowering under my dressing gown. Pepper, usually as brave as a lion!

"It was this movement of the dog's, I think, that gave me the first twinge of *real* fear. I had been considerably startled when the lights burnt first green and then red; but had been momentarily under the impression that the change was due to some influx of noxious gas into the room. Now, however, I saw that it was not so; for the candles burned with a steady flame, and showed no signs of going out, as would have been the case had the change been due to fumes in the atmosphere.

"I did not move. I felt distinctly frightened; but could think of nothing better to do than wait. For perhaps a minute, I kept my glance about the room, nervously. Then I noticed that the lights had commenced to sink, very slowly; until presently they showed minute specks of red fire, like the gleamings of rubies in the darkness. Still, I sat watching; while a sort of dreamy indifference seemed to steal over me; banishing altogether the fear that had begun to grip me.

"Away in the far end of the huge old-fashioned room, I became conscious of a faint glow. Steadily it grew, filling the room with gleams of quivering green light; then they sank quickly, and changed—even as the candle flames had done—into a deep, sombre crimson that strengthened, and lit up the room with a flood of awful glory.

"The light came from the end wall, and grew ever brighter until its intolerable glare caused my eyes acute pain, and involuntarily I closed them. It may have been a few seconds before I was able to open them. The first thing I noticed was that the light had decreased, greatly; so that it no longer tried my eyes. Then, as it grew still duller, I was aware, all at once, that, instead of looking at the redness, I was staring through it, and through the wall beyond.

"Gradually, as I became more accustomed to the idea, I realised that I was looking out on to a vast plain, lit with the same gloomy twilight that pervaded the room. The immensity of this plain scarcely can be conceived. In no part could I perceive its confines. It seemed to broaden and spread out, so that the eye failed to perceive any limitations. Slowly, the details of the nearer portions began to grow clear; then, in a moment almost, the light died away, and the vision—if vision it were—faded and was gone.

"Suddenly, I became conscious that I was no longer in the chair. Instead, I seemed to be hovering above it, and looking down at a dim something, huddled and silent. In a little while, a cold blast struck me, and I was outside in the night, floating, like a bubble, up through the darkness. As I moved, an icy coldness seemed to enfold me, so that I shivered.

"After a time, I looked to right and left, and saw the intolerable blackness of the night, pierced by remote gleams of fire. Onward, outward, I drove. Once, I glanced behind, and saw the earth, a small crescent of blue light, receding away to my left. Further off, the sun, a splash of white flame, burned vividly against the dark.

"An indefinite period passed. Then, for the last time, I saw the earth—an enduring globule of radiant blue, swimming in an eternity of ether. And there I, a fragile flake of soul dust, flickered silently across the void, from the distant blue, into the expanse of the unknown.

"A great while seemed to pass over me, and now I could nowhere see anything. I had passed beyond the fixed stars and plunged into the huge blackness that waits beyond. All this time I had experienced little, save a sense of lightness and cold discomfort. Now, however, the atrocious darkness seemed to creep into my soul, and I became filled with fear and despair. What was going to become of me? Where was I going? Even as the thoughts were formed, there grew against the impalpable blackness that wrapped me a faint tinge of blood. It seemed extraordinarily remote, and mist-like; yet, at once, the feeling of oppression was lightened, and I no longer despaired.

"Slowly, the distant redness became plainer and larger; until, as I drew nearer, it spread out into a great, sombre glare—dull and tremendous. Still, I fled onward, and, presently, I had come so close, that it seemed to stretch beneath me, like a great ocean of sombre red. I could see little, save that it appeared to spread out interminably in all directions.

"In a further space, I found that I was descending upon it; and, soon, I sank into a great sea of sullen, red-hued clouds. Slowly, I emerged from these, and there, below me, I saw the stupendous plain that I had seen from my room in this house that stands upon the borders of the Silences.

"Presently, I landed, and stood, surrounded by a great waste of loneliness. The place was lit with a gloomy twilight that gave an impression of indescribable desolation.

"Afar to my right, within the sky, there burnt a gigantic ring of dull-red fire, from the outer edge of which were projected huge, writhing flames, darted and jagged. The interior of this ring was black, black as the gloom of the outer night. I comprehended, at once, that it was from this extraordinary sun that the place derived its doleful light.

"From that strange source of light, I glanced down again to my surroundings. Everywhere I looked, I saw nothing but the same flat weariness of interminable plain. Nowhere could I descry any signs of life; not even the ruins of some ancient habitation.

"Gradually, I found that I was being borne forward, floating across the flat waste. For what seemed an eternity, I moved onward. I was unaware of any great sense of impatience; though some curiosity and a vast wonder were with me continually. Always, I saw around me the breadth of that enormous plain; and, always, I searched for some new thing to break its monotony; but there was no change—only loneliness, silence, and desert.

"Presently, in a half-conscious manner, I noticed that there was a faint mistiness, ruddy in hue, lying over its surface. Still, when I looked more intently, I was unable to say that it was really mist; for it appeared to blend with the plain, giving it a peculiar unrealness, and conveying to the senses the idea of unsubstantiality.

"Gradually, I began to weary with the sameness of the thing. Yet, it was a great time before I perceived any signs of the place, towards which I was being conveyed.

"At first, I saw it, far ahead, like a long hillock on the surface of the Plain. Then, as I drew nearer, I perceived that I had been mistaken; for, instead of a low hill, I made out, now, a chain of great mountains, whose distant peaks towered up into the red gloom, until they were almost lost to sight.

Chapter III
The House in the Arena

"And so, after a time, I came to the mountains. Then, the course of my journey was altered, and I began to move along their bases, until, all at once, I saw that I had come opposite to a vast rift, opening into the mountains. Through this, I was borne, moving at no great speed. On either side of me, huge, scarped walls of rocklike substance rose sheer. Far overhead, I discerned a thin ribbon of red, where the mouth of the chasm opened, among inaccessible peaks. Within, was gloom, deep and sombre, and chilly silence. For a while, I went onward steadily, and then, at last, I saw, ahead, a deep, red glow, that told me I was near upon the further opening of the gorge.

"A minute came and went, and I was at the exit of the chasm, staring out upon an enormous amphitheatre of mountains. Yet, of the mountains, and the terrible grandeur of the place, I recked nothing; for I was confounded with amazement to behold, at a distance of several miles and occupying the centre of the arena, a stupendous structure built apparently of green jade. Yet, in itself, it was not the discovery of the building that had so astonished me; but the fact, which became every moment more apparent, that in no particular, save in colour and its enormous size, did the lonely structure vary from this house in which I live.

"For a while, I continued to stare, fixedly. Even then, I could scarcely believe that I saw aright. In my mind, a question formed, reiterating incessantly: 'What does it mean?' 'What does it mean?' and I was unable to make answer, even out of the depths of my imagination. I seemed capable only of wonder and fear. For a time longer, I gazed, noting continually some fresh point of resemblance that attracted me. At last, wearied and sorely puzzled, I turned from it, to view the rest of the strange place on to which I had intruded.

"Hitherto, I had been so engrossed in my scrutiny of the House, that I had given only a cursory glance round. Now, as I looked, I began to realise upon what sort of a place I had come. The arena, for so I have termed it, appeared a perfect circle of about ten to twelve miles in diameter, the House, as I have mentioned before, standing in the centre. The surface of the place, like to that of the Plain, had a peculiar, misty appearance, that was yet not mist.

"From a rapid survey, my glance passed quickly upwards along the slopes of the circling mountains. How silent they were. I think that this same abominable stillness was more trying to me than anything that I had so far seen or imagined. I was looking up, now, at the great crags, towering so loftily. Up there, the impalpable redness gave a blurred appearance to everything.

"And then, as I peered, curiously, a new terror came to me; for away up among the dim peaks to my right, I had descried a vast shape of blackness, giant-like. It grew upon my sight. It had an enormous equine head, with gigantic ears, and seemed to peer steadfastly down into the arena. There was that about the pose that gave me the impression of an eternal watchfulness—of having warded that dismal place, through unknown eternities. Slowly, the monster became plainer to me; and then, suddenly, my gaze sprang from it to something further off and higher among the crags. For a long minute, I gazed, fearfully. I was strangely conscious of something not altogether unfamiliar—as though something stirred in the back of my mind. The thing was black, and had four grotesque arms. The features showed indistinctly. Round the neck, I made out several light-coloured objects. Slowly, the details came to me, and I realised, coldly, that they were skulls. Further down the body was another circling belt, showing less dark against the black trunk. Then, even as I puzzled to know what the thing was, a memory slid into my mind, and straightway, I knew that I was looking at a monstrous representation of Kali, the Hindu goddess of death.

"Other remembrances of my old student days drifted into my thoughts. My glance fell back upon the huge beast-headed Thing. Simultaneously, I recognised it for the ancient Egyptian god Set, or Seth, the Destroyer of Souls. With the knowledge, there came a great sweep of questioning—'Two of the—!' I stopped, and endeavoured to think. Things beyond my imagination peered into my frightened mind. I saw, obscurely. 'The old gods of mythology!' I tried to comprehend to what it was all pointing. My gaze dwelt, flickeringly, between the two. 'If—'

"An idea came swiftly, and I turned, and glanced rapidly upwards, searching the gloomy crags, away to my left. Something loomed out under a great peak, a shape of greyness. I wondered I had not seen it earlier, and then remembered I had not yet viewed that portion. I saw it more plainly now. It was, as I have said, grey. It had a tremendous head; but no eyes. That part of its face was blank.

"Now, I saw that there were other things up among the mountains. Further off, reclining on a lofty ledge, I made out a livid mass, irregular and ghoulish. It seemed without form, save for an unclean, half-animal face, that looked out, vilely, from somewhere about its middle. And then I saw others—there were hundreds of them. They seemed to grow out of the shadows. Several I recognised almost immediately as mythological deities; others were strange to me, utterly strange, beyond the power of a human mind to conceive.

"On each side, I looked, and saw more, continually. The mountains were full of strange things—Beast-gods, and Horrors so atrocious and bestial that possibility and decency deny any further attempt to describe them. And I—I was filled with a terrible sense of overwhelming horror and fear and repugnance; yet, spite of these, I wondered exceedingly. Was there then, after all, something in the old heathen worship, something more than the mere deifying of men, animals, and elements? The thought gripped me—was there?

"Later, a question repeated itself. What were they, those Beast-gods, and the others? At first, they had appeared to me just sculptured Monsters placed indiscriminately among the inaccessible peaks and precipices of the surrounding mountains. Now, as I scrutinised them with greater intentness, my mind began to reach out to fresh conclusions. There was something about them, an indescribable sort of silent vitality that suggested, to my broadening consciousness, a state of life-in-death—a something that was by no means life, as we understand it; but rather an inhuman form of existence, that well might be likened to a deathless trance—a condition in which it was possible to imagine their continuing, eternally. 'Immortal!' the word rose in my thoughts unbidden; and, straightway, I grew to wondering whether this might be the immortality of the gods.

"And then, in the midst of my wondering and musing, something happened. Until then, I had been staying just within the shadow of the exit of the great rift. Now, without volition on my part, I drifted out of the semi-darkness and began to move slowly across the arena—towards the

House. At this, I gave up all thoughts of those prodigious Shapes above me—and could only stare, frightenedly, at the tremendous structure towards which I was being conveyed so remorselessly. Yet, though I searched earnestly, I could discover nothing that I had not already seen, and so became gradually calmer.

"Presently, I had reached a point more than halfway between the House and the gorge. All around was spread the stark loneliness of the place, and the unbroken silence. Steadily, I neared the great building. Then, all at once, something caught my vision, something that came round one of the huge buttresses of the House, and so into full view. It was a gigantic thing, and moved with a curious lope, going almost upright, after the manner of a man. It was quite unclothed, and had a remarkable luminous appearance. Yet it was the face that attracted and frightened me the most. It was the face of a swine.

"Silently, intently, I watched this horrible creature, and forgot my fear, momentarily, in my interest in its movements. It was making its way, cumbrously round the building, stopping as it came to each window to peer in and shake at the bars, with which—as in this house—they were protected; and whenever it came to a door, it would push at it, fingering the fastening stealthily. Evidently, it was searching for an ingress into the House.

"I had come now to within less than a quarter of a mile of the great structure, and still I was compelled forward. Abruptly, the Thing turned and gazed hideously in my direction. It opened its mouth, and, for the first time, the stillness of that abominable place was broken, by a deep, booming note that sent an added thrill of apprehension through me. Then, immediately, I became aware that it was coming towards me, swiftly and silently. In an instant, it had covered half the distance that lay between. And still,

I was borne helplessly to meet it. Only a hundred yards, and the brutish ferocity of the giant face numbed me with a feeling of unmitigated horror. I could have screamed, in the supremeness of my fear; and then, in the very moment of my extremity and despair, I became conscious that I was looking down upon the arena, from a rapidly increasing height. I was rising, rising. In an inconceivably short while, I had reached an altitude of many hundred feet. Beneath me, the spot that I had just left, was occupied by the foul Swine-creature. It had gone down on all fours and was snuffing and rooting, like a veritable hog, at the surface of the arena. A moment and it rose to its feet, clutching upwards, with an expression of desire upon its face such as I have never seen in this world.

"Continually, I mounted higher. A few minutes, it seemed, and I had risen above the great mountains—floating, alone, afar in the redness. At a tremendous distance below, the arena showed, dimly; with the mighty House looking no larger than a tiny spot of green. The Swine-thing was no longer visible.

"Presently, I passed over the mountains, out above the huge breadth of the plain. Far away, on its surface, in the direction of the ring-shaped sun, there showed a confused blur. I looked towards it, indifferently. It reminded me, somewhat, of the first glimpse I had caught of the mountain-amphitheatre.

"With a sense of weariness, I glanced upwards at the immense ring of fire. What a strange thing it was! Then, as I stared, out from the dark centre, there spurted a sudden flare of extraordinary vivid fire. Compared with the size of the black centre, it was as naught; yet, in itself, stupendous. With awakened interest, I watched it carefully, noting its strange boiling and glowing. Then, in a moment, the whole thing grew dim and unreal, and so passed out of sight. Much amazed, I glanced down to the Plain from which I was still rising. Thus, I received a fresh surprise. The Plain—everything had vanished, and only a sea of red mist was spread far below me. Gradually as I stared this grew remote, and died away into a dim far mystery of red against an unfathomable night. A while, and even this had gone, and I was wrapped in an impalpable, lightless gloom.

Chapter IV
The Earth

"Thus I was, and only the memory that I had lived through the dark, once before, served to sustain my thoughts. A great time passed—ages. And then a single star broke its way through the darkness. It was the first of one of the outlying clusters of this universe. Presently, it was far behind, and all about me shone the splendour of the countless stars. Later, years it seemed, I saw the sun, a clot of flame. Around it, I made out presently several remote specks of light—the planets of the Solar system. And so I saw the earth again, blue and unbelievably minute. It grew larger, and became defined.

"A long space of time came and went, and then at last I entered into the shadow of the world—plunging headlong into the dim and holy earth night. Overhead were the old constellations, and there was a crescent moon. Then, as I neared the earth's surface, a dimness swept over me, and I appeared to sink into a black mist.

"For awhile, I knew nothing. I was unconscious. Gradually, I became aware of a faint, distant whining. It became plainer. A desperate feeling of agony possessed me. I struggled madly for breath, and tried to shout. A moment, and I got my breath more easily. I was conscious that something was licking my hand. Something damp swept across my face. I heard a panting, and then again the whining. It seemed to come to my ears, now, with a sense of familiarity, and I opened my eyes. All was dark; but the feeling of oppression had left me. I was seated, and something was whining piteously, and licking me. I felt strangely confused, and, instinctively, tried to ward off the thing that licked. My head was curiously vacant, and, for the moment, I seemed incapable of action or thought. Then, things came back to me, and I called 'Pepper,' faintly. I was answered by a joyful bark, and renewed and frantic caresses.

"In a little while, I felt stronger, and put out my hand for the matches. I groped about, for a few moments, blindly; then my hands lit upon them, and I struck a light, and looked confusedly around. All about me, I saw the old, familiar things. And there I sat, full of dazed wonders, until the flame of the match burnt my finger, and I dropped it; while a hasty expression of pain and anger, escaped my lips, surprising me with the sound of my own voice.

"After a moment, I struck another match, and, stumbling across the room, lit the candles. As I did so, I observed that they had not burned away, but had been put out.

"As the flames shot up, I turned, and stared about the study; yet there was nothing unusual to see; and, suddenly, a gust of irritation took me. What had happened? I held my head, with both hands, and tried to remember. Ah! the great, silent Plain, and the ring-shaped sun of red fire. Where were they? Where had I seen them? How long ago? I felt dazed and muddled. Once or twice, I walked up and down the room, unsteadily. My memory seemed dulled, and, already, the thing I had witnessed came back to me with an effort.

"I have a remembrance of cursing, peevishly, in my bewilderment. Suddenly, I turned faint and giddy, and had to grasp at the table for support. During a few moments, I held on, weakly; and then managed to totter sideways into a chair. After a little time, I felt somewhat better, and succeeded in reaching the cupboard where, usually, I keep brandy and biscuits. I poured myself out a little of the stimulant, and drank it off. Then, taking a handful of biscuits, I returned to my chair, and began to devour them, ravenously. I was vaguely surprised at my hunger. I felt as though I had eaten nothing for an uncountably long while.

"As I ate, my glance roved about the room, taking in its various details, and still searching, though almost unconsciously, for something tangible upon which to take hold, among the invisible mysteries that encompassed me. 'Surely,' I thought, 'there must be something—' And, in the same instant, my gaze dwelt upon the face of the clock in the opposite corner. Therewith, I stopped eating, and just stared. For, though its ticking indicated most certainly that it was still going, the hands were pointing to a little *before* the hour of midnight; whereas it was, as well I knew, considerably *after* that time when I had witnessed the first of the strange happenings I have just described.

"For perhaps a moment I was astounded and puzzled. Had the hour been the same as when I had last seen the clock, I should have concluded that the hands had stuck in one place, while the internal mechanism went on as usual; but that would, in no way, account for the hands having travelled backwards. Then, even as I turned the matter over in my wearied brain, the thought flashed upon me that it was now close upon the morning of the twenty-second, and that I had been unconscious to the visible world through the greater portion of the last twenty-four hours. The thought occupied my attention for a full minute; then I commenced to eat again. I was still very hungry.

"During breakfast, next morning, I inquired casually of my sister regarding the date, and found my surmise correct. I had, indeed, been absent—at least in spirit—for nearly a day and a night.

"My sister asked me no questions; for it is not by any means the first time that I have kept to my study for a whole day, and sometimes a couple of days at a time, when I have been particularly engrossed in my books or work.

"And so the days pass on, and I am still filled with a wonder to know the meaning of all that I saw on that memorable night. Yet, well I know that my curiosity is little likely to be satisfied.

Chapter V
The Thing in the Pit

"This house is, as I have said before, surrounded by a huge estate, and wild and uncultivated gardens.

"Away at the back, distant some three hundred yards, is a dark, deep ravine—spoken of as the 'Pit,' by the peasantry. At the bottom runs a sluggish stream so overhung by trees as scarcely to be seen from above.

"In passing, I must explain that this river has a subterranean origin, emerging suddenly at the East end of the ravine, and disappearing, as abruptly, beneath the cliffs that form its Western extremity.

"It was some months after my vision (if vision it were) of the great Plain that my attention was particularly attracted to the Pit.

"I happened, one day, to be walking along its Southern edge, when, suddenly, several pieces of rock and shale were dislodged from the face of the cliff immediately beneath me, and fell with a sullen crash through the trees. I heard them splash in the river at the bottom; and then silence. I should not have given this incident more than a passing thought, had not Pepper at once begun to bark savagely; nor would he be silent when I bade him, which is most unusual behaviour on his part.

"Feeling that there must be someone or something in the Pit, I went back to the house, quickly, for a stick. When

I returned, Pepper had ceased his barks and was growling and smelling, uneasily, along the top.

"Whistling to him to follow me, I started to descend cautiously. The depth to the bottom of the Pit must be about a hundred and fifty feet, and some time as well as considerable care was expended before we reached the bottom in safety.

"Once down, Pepper and I started to explore along the banks of the river. It was very dark there due to the overhanging trees, and I moved warily, keeping my glance about me and my stick ready.

"Pepper was quiet now and kept close to me all the time. Thus, we searched right up one side of the river, without hearing or seeing anything. Then, we crossed over—by the simple method of jumping—and commenced to beat our way back through the underbrush.

"We had accomplished perhaps half the distance, when I heard again the sound of falling stones on the other side— the side from which we had just come. One large rock came thundering down through the treetops, struck the opposite bank, and bounded into the river, driving a great jet of water right over us. At this, Pepper gave out a deep growl; then stopped, and pricked up his ears. I listened, also.

"A second later, a loud, half-human, half-pig-like squeal sounded from among the trees, apparently about halfway up the South cliff. It was answered by a similar note from the bottom of the Pit. At this, Pepper gave a short, sharp bark, and, springing across the little river, disappeared into the bushes.

"Immediately afterwards, I heard his barks increase in depth and number, and in between there sounded a noise of confused jabbering. This ceased, and, in the succeeding silence, there rose a semi-human yell of agony. Almost immediately, Pepper gave a long-drawn howl of pain, and then the shrubs were violently agitated, and he came running out with his tail down, and glancing as he ran over his shoulder. As he reached me, I saw that he was bleeding from what appeared to be a great claw wound in the side that had almost laid bare his ribs.

"Seeing Pepper thus mutilated, a furious feeling of anger seized me, and, whirling my staff, I sprang across, and into the bushes from which Pepper had emerged. As I forced my way through, I thought I heard a sound of breathing. Next instant, I had burst into a little clear space, just in time to see something, livid white in colour, disappear among the bushes on the opposite side. With a shout, I ran towards it; but, though I struck and probed among the bushes with my stick, I neither saw nor heard anything further; and so returned to Pepper. There, after bathing his wound in the river, I bound my wetted handkerchief round his body; having done which, we retreated up the ravine and into the daylight again.

"On reaching the house, my sister inquired what had happened to Pepper, and I told her he had been fighting with a wildcat, of which I had heard there were several about.

"I felt it would be better not to tell her how it had really happened; though, to be sure, I scarcely knew myself; but this I did know, that the thing I had seen run into the bushes was no wildcat. It was much too big, and had, so far as I had observed, a skin like a hog's, only of a dead, unhealthy white colour. And then—it had run upright, or nearly so, upon its hind feet, with a motion somewhat resembling that of a human being. This much I had noticed in my brief glimpse, and, truth to tell, I felt a good deal of uneasiness, besides curiosity as I turned the matter over in my mind.

"It was in the morning that the above incident had occurred.

"Then, it would be after dinner, as I sat reading, that, happening to look up suddenly, I saw something peering in over the window ledge the eyes and ears alone showing.

" 'A pig, by Jove!' I said, and rose to my feet. Thus, I saw the thing more completely; but it was no pig—God alone knows what it was. It reminded me, vaguely, of the hideous Thing that had haunted the great arena. It had a grotesquely human mouth and jaw; but with no chin of which to speak. The nose was prolonged into a snout; this it was, that, with the little eyes and queer ears, gave it such an extraordinarily swine-like appearance. Of forehead there was little, and the whole face was of an unwholesome white colour.

"For perhaps a minute, I stood looking at the thing with an ever growing feeling of disgust, and some fear. The mouth kept jabbering, inanely, and once emitted a half-swinish grunt. I think it was the eyes that attracted me the most; they seemed to glow, at times, with a horribly human intelligence, and kept flickering away from my face, over the details of the room, as though my stare disturbed it.

"It appeared to be supporting itself by two claw-like hands upon the windowsill. These claws, unlike the face, were of a clayey brown hue, and bore an indistinct resemblance to human hands, in that they had four fingers and a thumb; though these were webbed up to the first joint, much as are a duck's. Nails it had also, but so long and powerful that they were more like the talons of an eagle than aught else.

"As I have said, before, I felt some fear; though almost of an impersonal kind. I may explain my feeling better by saying that it was more a sensation of abhorrence; such as one might expect to feel, if brought in contact with something superhumanly foul; something unholy—belonging to some hitherto undreamt of state of existence.

"I cannot say that I grasped these various details of the brute at the time. I think they seemed to come back to me, afterwards, as though imprinted upon my brain. I imagined more than I saw as I looked at the thing, and the material details grew upon me later.

"For perhaps a minute I stared at the creature; then as my nerves steadied a little I shook off the vague alarm that held me, and took a step towards the window. Even as I did so, the thing ducked and vanished. I rushed to the door and looked round hurriedly; but only the tangled bushes and shrubs met my gaze.

"I ran back into the house, and, getting my gun, sallied out to search through the gardens. As I went, I asked myself whether the thing I had just seen was likely to be the same of which I had caught a glimpse in the morning. I inclined to think it was.

"I would have taken Pepper with me; but judged it better to give his wound a chance to heal. Besides, if the creature I had just seen was, as I imagined, his antagonist of the morning, it was not likely that he would be of much use.

"I began my search, systematically. I was determined, if it were possible, to find and put an end to that swine-thing. This was, at least, a material Horror!

"At first, I searched, cautiously; with the thought of Pepper's wound in my mind; but, as the hours passed, and not a sign of anything living, showed in the great, lonely gardens, I became less apprehensive. I felt almost as though I would welcome the sight of it. Anything seemed better than this silence, with the ever-present feeling that the creature might be lurking in every bush I passed. Later, I grew careless of danger, to the extent of plunging right through the bushes, probing with my gun barrel as I went.

"At times, I shouted; but only the echoes answered back. I thought thus perhaps to frighten or stir the creature to showing itself; but only succeeded in bringing my sister Mary out, to know what was the matter. I told her, that I had seen the wildcat that had wounded Pepper, and that I was trying to hunt it out of the bushes. She seemed only half satisfied, and went back into the house, with an expression of doubt upon her face. I wondered whether she had seen or guessed anything. For the rest of the afternoon, I prosecuted the search anxiously. I felt that I should be unable to sleep, with that bestial thing haunting the shrubberies, and yet, when evening fell, I had seen nothing. Then, as I turned homewards, I heard a short, unintelligible noise, among the bushes to my right. Instantly, I turned, and, aiming quickly, fired in the direction of the sound. Immediately afterwards, I heard something scuttling away among the bushes. It moved rapidly, and in a minute had gone out of hearing. After a few steps I ceased my pursuit, realising how futile it must be in the fast gathering gloom; and so, with a curious feeling of depression, I entered the house.

"That night, after my sister had gone to bed, I went round to all the windows and doors on the ground floor; and saw to it that they were securely fastened. This precaution was scarcely necessary as regards the windows, as all of those on the lower storey are strongly barred; but with the doors—of which there are five—it was wisely thought, as not one was locked.

"Having secured these, I went to my study, yet, somehow, for once, the place jarred upon me; it seemed so huge and echoey. For some time I tried to read; but at last finding it impossible I carried my book down to the kitchen where a large fire was burning, and sat there.

"I dare say, I had read for a couple of hours, when, suddenly, I heard a sound that made me lower my book, and listen, intently. It was a noise of something rubbing and fumbling against the back door. Once the door creaked, loudly; as though force were being applied to it. During those few, short moments, I experienced an indescribable feeling of terror, such as I should have believed impossible. My hands shook; a cold sweat broke out on me, and I shivered violently.

"Gradually, I calmed. The stealthy movements outside had ceased.

"Then for an hour I sat silent and watchful. All at once the feeling of fear took me again. I felt as I imagine an animal must, under the eye of a snake. Yet now I could hear nothing. Still, there was no doubting that some unexplained influence was at work.

"Gradually, imperceptibly almost, something stole on my ear—a sound that resolved itself into a faint murmur. Quickly it developed and grew into a muffled but hideous chorus of bestial shrieks. It appeared to rise from the bowels of the earth.

"I heard a thud, and realised in a dull, half comprehending way that I had dropped my book. After that, I just sat; and thus the daylight found me, when it crept wanly in through the barred, high windows of the great kitchen.

"With the dawning light, the feeling of stupor and fear left me; and I came more into possession of my senses.

"Thereupon I picked up my book, and crept to the door to listen. Not a sound broke the chilly silence. For some minutes I stood there; then, very gradually and cautiously, I drew back the bolt and opening the door peeped out.

"My caution was unneeded. Nothing was to be seen, save the grey vista of dreary, tangled bushes and trees, extending to the distant plantation.

"With a shiver, I closed the door, and made my way, quietly, up to bed.

Chapter VI
The Swine-Things

"It was evening, a week later. My sister sat in the garden, knitting. I was walking up and down, reading. My gun leant up against the wall of the house; for, since the advent of that strange thing in the gardens, I had deemed it wise to take precautions. Yet, through the whole week, there had been nothing to alarm me, either by sight or sound; so that I was able to look back, calmly, to the incident; though still with a sense of unmitigated wonder and curiosity.

"I was, as I have just said, walking up and down, and somewhat engrossed in my book. Suddenly, I heard a crash, away in the direction of the Pit. With a quick movement, I turned and saw a tremendous column of dust rising high into the evening air.

"My sister had risen to her feet, with a sharp exclamation of surprise and fright.

"Telling her to stay where she was, I snatched up my gun, and ran towards the Pit. As I neared it, I heard a dull, rumbling sound, that grew quickly into a roar, split with deeper crashes, and up from the Pit drove a fresh volume of dust.

"The noise ceased, though the dust still rose, tumultuously.

"I reached the edge, and looked down; but could see nothing save a boil of dust clouds swirling hither and thither. The air was so full of the small particles, that they blinded and choked me; and, finally, I had to run out from the smother, to breathe.

"Gradually, the suspended matter sank, and hung in a panoply over the mouth of the Pit.

"I could only guess at what had happened.

"That there had been a land-slip of some kind, I had little doubt; but the cause was beyond my knowledge; and yet, even then, I had half imaginings; for, already, the thought had come to me, of those falling rocks, and that Thing in the bottom of the Pit; but, in the first minutes of confusion, I failed to reach the natural conclusion, to which the catastrophe pointed.

"Slowly, the dust subsided, until, presently, I was able to approach the edge, and look down.

"For a while, I peered impotently, trying to see through the reek. At first, it was impossible to make out anything. Then, as I stared, I saw something below, to my left, that moved. I looked intently towards it, and, presently, made out another, and then another—three dim shapes that appeared to be climbing up the side of the Pit. I could see them only indistinctly. Even as I stared and wondered, I heard a rattle of stones, somewhere to my right. I glanced across; but could see nothing. I leant forward, and peered over, and down into the Pit, just beneath where I stood; and saw no further than a hideous, white swine-face, that had risen to within a couple of yards of my feet. Below it, I could make out several others. As the Thing saw me, it gave a sudden, uncouth squeal, which was answered from all parts of the Pit. At that, a gust of horror and fear took me, and, bending down, I discharged my gun right into its face. Straightway, the creature disappeared, with a clatter of loose earth and stones.

"There was a momentary silence, to which, probably, I owe my life; for, during it, I heard a quick patter of many feet, and, turning sharply, saw a troop of the creatures coming towards me, at a run. Instantly, I raised my gun and fired at the foremost, who plunged head-long, with a hideous howling. Then, I turned to run. More than halfway from the house to the Pit, I saw my sister—she was coming towards me. I could not see her face, distinctly, as the dusk had fallen; but there was fear in her voice as she called to know why I was shooting.

" 'Run!' I shouted in reply. 'Run for your life!'

"Without more ado, she turned and fled—picking up her skirts with both hands. As I followed, I gave a glance behind. The brutes were running on their hind legs—at times dropping on all fours.

"I think it must have been the terror in my voice, that spurred Mary to run so; for I feel convinced that she had not, as yet, seen those hell creatures that pursued.

"On we went, my sister leading.

"Each moment, the nearing sounds of the footsteps, told me that the brutes were gaining on us, rapidly. Fortunately, I am accustomed to live, in some ways, an active life. As it was, the strain of the race was beginning to tell severely upon me.

"Ahead, I could see the back door—luckily it was open. I was some half-dozen yards behind Mary, now, and my breath was sobbing in my throat. Then, something touched my shoulder. I wrenched my head round, quickly, and saw one of those monstrous, pallid faces close to mine. One of the creatures, having outrun its companions, had almost overtaken me. Even as I turned, it made a fresh grab. With a sudden effort, I sprang to one side, and, swinging my gun by the barrel, brought it crashing down upon the foul creature's head. The Thing dropped, with an almost human groan.

"Even this short delay had been nearly sufficient to bring the rest of the brutes down upon me; so that, without an instant's waste of time, I turned and ran for the door.

"Reaching it, I burst into the passage; then, turning quickly, slammed and bolted the door, just as the first of the creatures rushed against it, with a sudden shock.

"My sister sat, gasping, in a chair. She seemed in a fainting condition; but I had no time then to spend on her. I had to make sure that all the doors were fastened. Fortunately, they were. The one leading from my study into the gardens, was the last to which I went. I had just had time to note that it was secured, when I thought I heard a noise outside. I stood perfectly silent, and listened. Yes! Now I could distinctly hear a sound of whispering, and something slithered over the panels, with a rasping, scratchy noise. Evidently, some of the brutes were feeling with their claw-hands, about the door, to discover whether there were any means of ingress.

"That the creatures should so soon have found the door was—to me—a proof of their reasoning capabilities. It assured me that they must not be regarded, by any means, as mere animals. I had felt something of this before, when that first Thing peered in through my window. Then I had applied the term superhuman to it, with an almost instinctive knowledge that the creature was something different from the brute-beast. Something beyond human; yet in no good sense; but rather as something foul and hostile to the *great* and *good* in humanity. In a word, as something intelligent, and yet inhuman. The very thought of the creatures filled me with revulsion.

"Now, I bethought me of my sister, and, going to the cupboard, I got out a flask of brandy, and a wineglass. Taking these, I went down to the kitchen, carrying a lighted candle with me. She was not sitting in the chair, but had fallen out, and was lying upon the floor, face downwards.

"Very gently, I turned her over, and raised her head somewhat. Then, I poured a little of the brandy between her lips. After a while, she shivered slightly. A little later, she gave several gasps, and opened her eyes. In a dreamy, unrealising way, she looked at me. Then her eyes closed, slowly, and I gave her a little more of the brandy. For, perhaps a minute longer, she lay silent, breathing quickly. All at once, her eyes opened again, and it seemed to me, as I looked, that the pupils were dilated, as though fear had come with returning consciousness. Then, with a movement so unexpected that I started backwards, she sat up. Noticing that she seemed giddy, I put out my hand to steady her. At that, she gave a loud scream, and, scrambling to her feet, ran from the room.

"For a moment, I stayed there—kneeling and holding the brandy flask. I was utterly puzzled and astonished.

"Could she be afraid of me? But no! Why should she? I could only conclude that her nerves were badly shaken, and that she was temporarily unhinged. Upstairs, I heard a door bang, loudly, and I knew that she had taken refuge in her room. I put the flask down on the table. My attention was distracted by a noise in the direction of the back door. I went towards it, and listened. It appeared to be shaken, as though some of the creatures struggled with it, silently; but it was far too strongly constructed and hung to be easily moved.

"Out in the gardens rose a continuous sound. It might have been mistaken, by a casual listener, for the grunting and squealing of a herd of pigs. But, as I stood there, it came to me that there was sense and meaning to all those swinish noises. Gradually, I seemed able to trace a semblance in it to human speech—glutinous and sticky, as though each articulation were made with difficulty: yet, nevertheless, I was becoming convinced that it was no mere medley of sounds; but a rapid interchange of ideas.

"By this time, it had grown quite dark in the passages, and from these came all the varied cries and groans of which an old house is so full after nightfall. It is, no doubt, because things are then quieter, and one has more leisure to hear. Also, there may be something in the theory that the sudden change of temperature, at sundown, affects the structure of the house, somewhat—causing it to contract and settle, as it were, for the night. However, this is as may be; but, on that night in particular, I would gladly have been quit of so many eerie noises. It seemed to me, that each crack and creak was the coming of one of those Things along the dark corridors; though I knew in my heart that this could not be, for I had seen, myself, that all the doors were secure.

"Gradually, however, these sounds grew on my nerves to such an extent that, were it only to punish my cowardice, I felt I must make the round of the basement again, and, if anything were there, face it. And then, I would go up to my study, for I knew sleep was out of the question, with the house surrounded by creatures, half beasts, half something else, and entirely unholy.

"Taking the kitchen lamp down from its hook, I made my way from cellar to cellar, and room to room; through pantry and coal-hole—along passages, and into the hundred-and-one little blind alleys and hidden nooks that form the basement of the old house. Then, when I knew I had been in every corner and cranny large enough to conceal aught of any size, I made my way to the stairs.

"With my foot on the first step, I paused. It seemed to me, I heard a movement, apparently from the buttery, which is to the left of the staircase. It had been one of the first places I searched, and yet, I felt certain my ears had not deceived me. My nerves were strung now, and, with hardly any hesitation, I stepped up to the door, holding the lamp above my head. In a glance, I saw that the place was empty, save for the heavy, stone slabs, supported by brick pillars; and I was about to leave it, convinced that I had been mistaken; when, in turning, my light was flashed back from two bright spots outside the window, and high up. For a few moments, I stood there, staring. Then they moved—revolving slowly, and throwing out alternate scintillations of green and red; at least, so it appeared to me. I knew then that they were eyes.

"Slowly, I traced the shadowy outline of one of the Things. It appeared to be holding on to the bars of the window, and its attitude suggested climbing. I went nearer to the window, and held the light higher. There was no need to be afraid of the creature; the bars were strong, and there was little danger of its being able to move them. And then, suddenly, in spite of the knowledge that the brute could not reach to harm me, I had a return of the horrible sensation of fear, that had assailed me on that night, a week previously. It was the same feeling of helpless, shuddering fright. I realised, dimly, that the creature's eyes were looking into mine with a steady, compelling stare. I tried to turn away; but could not. I seemed, now, to see the window through a mist. Then, I thought other eyes came and peered, and yet others; until a whole galaxy of malignant, staring orbs seemed to hold me in thrall.

"My head began to swim, and throb violently. Then, I was aware of a feeling of acute physical pain in my left hand. It grew more severe, and forced, literally forced, my attention. With a tremendous effort, I glanced down; and, with that, the spell that had held me was broken. I realised, then, that I had, in my agitation, unconsciously caught hold of the hot lamp-glass, and burnt my hand, badly. I looked up to the window, again. The misty appearance had gone, and, now, I saw that it was crowded with dozens of bestial faces. With a sudden access of rage, I raised the lamp, and hurled it, full at the window. It struck the glass (smashing a pane), and passed between two of the bars, out into the garden, scattering burning oil as it went. I heard several loud cries of pain, and, as my sight became accustomed to the dark, I discovered that the creatures had left the window.

"Pulling myself together, I groped for the door, and, having found it, made my way upstairs, stumbling at each step. I felt dazed, as though I had received a blow on the head. At the same time, my hand smarted badly, and I was full of a nervous, dull rage against those Things.

"Reaching my study, I lit the candles. As they burnt up, their rays were reflected from the rack of firearms on the sidewall. At the sight, I remembered that I had there a power, which, as I had proved earlier, seemed as fatal to those monsters as to more ordinary animals; and I determined I would take the offensive.

"First of all, I bound up my hand; for the pain was fast becoming intolerable. After that, it seemed easier, and I crossed the room, to the rifle stand. There, I selected a heavy rifle—an old and tried weapon; and, having procured ammunition, I made my way up into one of the small towers, with which the house is crowned.

"From there, I found that I could see nothing. The gardens presented a dim blur of shadows—a little blacker, perhaps, where the trees stood. That was all, and I knew that it was useless to shoot down into all that darkness. The only thing to be done, was to wait for the moon to rise; then, I might be able to do a little execution.

"In the meantime, I sat still, and kept my ears open. The gardens were comparatively quiet now, and only an occasional grunt or squeal came up to me. I did not like this silence; it made me wonder on what devilry the creatures were bent. Twice, I left the tower, and took a walk through the house; but everything was silent.

"Once, I heard a noise, from the direction of the Pit, as though more earth had fallen. Following this, and lasting for some fifteen minutes, there was a commotion among the denizens of the gardens. This died away, and, after that all was again quiet.

"About an hour later, the moon's light showed above the distant horizon. From where I sat, I could see it over the trees; but it was not until it rose clear of them, that I could make out any of the details in the gardens below. Even then, I could see none of the brutes; until, happening to crane forward, I saw several of them lying prone, up against the wall of the house. What they were doing, I could not make out. It was, however, a chance too good to be ignored; and, taking aim, I fired at the one directly beneath. There was a shrill scream, and, as the smoke cleared away, I saw that it had turned on its back, and was writhing, feebly. Then, it was quiet. The others had disappeared.

"Immediately after this, I heard a loud squeal, in the direction of the Pit. It was answered, a hundred times, from every part of the garden. This gave me some notion of the number of the creatures, and I began to feel that the whole affair was becoming even more serious than I had imagined.

"As I sat there, silent and watchful, the thought came to me—Why was all this? What were these Things? What did it mean? Then my thoughts flew back to that vision (though, even now, I doubt whether it was a vision) of the Plain of Silence. What did that mean? I wondered—And that Thing in the arena? Ugh! Lastly, I thought of the house I had seen in that far-away place. That house, so like this in every detail of external structure, that it might have been modelled from it; or this from that. I had never thought of that—

"At this moment, there came another long squeal, from the Pit, followed, a second later, by a couple of shorter ones. At once, the garden was filled with answering cries. I stood up, quickly, and looked over the parapet. In the moonlight, it seemed as though the shrubberies were alive. They tossed hither and thither, as though shaken by a strong, irregular wind; while a continuous rustling, and a noise of scampering feet, rose up to me. Several times, I saw the moonlight gleam on running, white figures among the bushes, and, twice, I fired. The second time, my shot was answered by a short squeal of pain.

"A minute later, the gardens lay silent. From the Pit, came a deep, hoarse Babel of swine-talk. At times, angry cries smote the air, and they would be answered by multitudinous gruntings. It occurred to me, that they were holding some kind of a council, perhaps to discuss the problem of entering the house. Also, I thought that they seemed much enraged, probably by my successful shots.

"It occurred to me, that now would be a good time to make a final survey of our defences. This, I proceeded to do at once; visiting the whole of the basement again, and examining each of the doors. Luckily, they are all, like the back one, built of solid, iron-studded oak. Then, I went upstairs to the study. I was more anxious about this door. It is, palpably, of a more modern make than the others, and, though a stout piece of work, it has little of their ponderous strength.

"I must explain here, that there is a small, raised lawn on this side of the house, upon which this door opens—the windows of the study being barred on this account. All the other entrances—excepting the great gateway which is never opened—are in the lower storey.

Chapter VII
The Attack

"I spent some time, puzzling how to strengthen the study door. Finally, I went down to the kitchen, and with some trouble, brought up several heavy pieces of timber. These, I wedged up, slantwise, against it, from the floor, nailing them top and bottom. For half-an-hour, I worked hard, and, at last, got it shored to my mind.

"Then, feeling easier, I resumed my coat, which I had laid aside, and proceeded to attend to one or two matters before returning to the tower. It was whilst thus employed, that I heard a fumbling at the door, and the latch was tried. Keeping silence, I waited. Soon, I heard several of the creatures outside. They were grunting to one another, softly. Then, for a minute, there was quietness. Suddenly, there sounded a quick, low grunt, and the door creaked under a tremendous pressure. It would have burst inwards; but for the supports I had placed. The strain ceased, as quickly as it had begun, and there was more talk.

"Presently, one of the Things squealed, softly, and I heard the sound of others approaching. There was a short confabulation; then again, silence; and I realised that they had called several more to assist. Feeling that now was the supreme moment, I stood ready, with my rifle presented. If the door gave, I would, at least, slay as many as possible.

"Again came the low signal; and, once more, the door cracked, under a huge force. For, a minute perhaps, the pressure was kept up; and I waited, nervously; expecting each moment to see the door come down with a crash. But no; the struts held, and the attempt proved abortive. Then followed more of their horrible, grunting talk, and, whilst it lasted, I thought I distinguished the noise of fresh arrivals.

"After a long discussion, during which the door was several times shaken, they became quiet once more, and I knew that they were going to make a third attempt to break it down. I was almost in despair. The props had been severely tried in the two previous attacks, and I was sorely afraid that this would prove too much for them.

"At that moment, like an inspiration, a thought flashed into my troubled brain. Instantly, for it was no time to hesitate, I ran from the room, and up stair after stair. This time, it was not to one of the towers, that I went; but out on to the flat, leaded roof itself. Once there, I raced across to the parapet, that walls it round, and looked down. As I did so, I heard the short, grunted signal, and, even up there, caught the crying of the door under the assault.

"There was not a moment to lose, and, leaning over, I aimed, quickly, and fired. The report rang sharply, and, almost blending with it, came the loud splud of the bullet striking its mark. From below, rose a shrill wail; and the door ceased its groaning. Then, as I took my weight from off the parapet, a huge piece of the stone coping slid from under me, and fell with a crash among the disorganised throng beneath. Several horrible shrieks quavered through the night air, and then I heard a sound of scampering feet. Cautiously, I looked over. In the moonlight, I could see the great coping stone, lying right across the threshold of the door. I thought I saw something under it—several things, white; but I could not be sure.

"And so a few minutes passed.

"As I stared, I saw something come round, out of the shadow of the house. It was one of the Things. It went up to the stone, silently, and bent down. I was unable to see what it did. In a minute it stood up. It had something in its talons, which it put to its mouth and tore at . . . .

"For the moment, I did not realise. Then, slowly, I comprehended. The Thing was stooping again. It was horrible. I started to load my rifle. When I looked again, the monster was tugging at the stone—moving it to one side. I leant the rifle on the coping, and pulled the trigger. The brute collapsed, on its face, and kicked, slightly.

"Simultaneously, almost, with the report, I heard another sound—that of breaking glass. Waiting, only to recharge my weapon, I ran from the roof, and down the first two flights of stairs.

"Here, I paused to listen. As I did so, there came another tinkle of falling glass. It appeared to come from the floor below. Excitedly, I sprang down the steps, and, guided by the rattle of the window-sash, reached the door of one of the empty bedrooms, at the back of the house. I thrust it open. The room was but dimly illuminated by the moonlight; most of the light being blotted out by moving figures at the window. Even as I stood, one crawled through, into the room. Levelling my weapon, I fired point-blank at it—filling the room with a deafening bang. When the smoke cleared, I saw that the room was empty, and the window free. The room was much lighter. The night air blew in, coldly, through the shattered panes. Down below, in the night, I could hear a soft moaning, and a confused murmur of swine-voices.

"Stepping to one side of the window, I reloaded, and then stood there, waiting. Presently, I heard a scuffling noise. From where I stood in the shadow, I could see, without being seen.

"Nearer came the sounds, and then I saw something come up above the sill, and clutch at the broken window-frame. It caught a piece of the woodwork; and, now, I could make out that it was a hand and arm. A moment later, the face of one of the Swine-creatures rose into view. Then, before I could use my rifle, or do anything, there came a sharp crack—cr-a-c-k; and the window-frame gave way under the weight of the Thing. Next instant, a squashing thud, and a loud outcry, told me that it had fallen to the ground. With a savage hope that it had been killed, I went to the window. The moon had gone behind a cloud, so that I could see nothing; though a steady hum of jabbering, just beneath where I stood, indicated that there were several more of the brutes close at hand.

"As I stood there, looking down, I marvelled how it had been possible for the creatures to climb so far; for the wall is comparatively smooth, while the distance to the ground must be, at least, eighty feet.

"All at once, as I bent, peering, I saw something, indistinctly, that cut the grey shadow of the house-side, with a black line. It passed the window, to the left, at a distance of about two feet. Then, I remembered that it was a gutter-pipe, that had been put there some years ago, to carry off the rainwater. I had forgotten about it. I could see, now, how the creatures had managed to reach the window. Even as the solution came to me, I heard a faint slithering, scratching noise, and knew that another of the brutes was coming. I waited some odd moments; then leant out of the window and felt the pipe. To my delight, I found that it was quite loose, and I managed, using the rifle-barrel as a crowbar, to lever it out from the wall. I worked quickly. Then, taking hold with both hands, I wrenched the whole concern away, and hurled it down—with the Thing still clinging to it—into the garden.

"For a few minutes longer, I waited there, listening; but, after the first general outcry, I heard nothing. I knew, now, that there was no more reason to fear an attack from this quarter. I had removed the only means of reaching the window, and, as none of the other windows had any adjacent water pipes, to tempt the climbing powers of the monsters, I began to feel more confident of escaping their clutches.

"Leaving the room, I made my way down to the study. I was anxious to see how the door had withstood the test of that last assault. Entering, I lit two of the candles, and then turned to the door. One of the large props had been displaced, and, on that side, the door had been forced inwards some six inches.

"It was Providential that I had managed to drive the brutes away just when I did! And that copingstone! I wondered, vaguely, how I had managed to dislodge it. I had not noticed it loose, as I took my shot; and then, as I stood up, it had slipped away from beneath me . . . . I felt that I owed the dismissal of the attacking force, more to its timely fall than to my rifle. Then the thought came, that I had better seize this chance to shore up the door, again. It was evident that the creatures had not returned since the fall of the copingstone; but who was to say how long they would keep away?

"There and then, I set-to, at repairing the door—working hard and anxiously. First, I went down to the basement, and, rummaging round, found several pieces of heavy oak planking. With these, I returned to the study, and, having removed the props, placed the planks up against the door. Then, I nailed the heads of the struts to these, and, driving them well home at the bottoms, nailed them again there.

"Thus, I made the door stronger than ever; for now it was solid with the backing of boards, and would, I felt convinced, stand a heavier pressure than hitherto, without giving way.

"After that, I lit the lamp which I had brought from the kitchen, and went down to have a look at the lower windows.

"Now that I had seen an instance of the strength the creatures possessed, I felt considerable anxiety about the windows on the ground floor—in spite of the fact that they were so strongly barred.

"I went first to the buttery, having a vivid remembrance of my late adventure there. The place was chilly, and the wind, soughing in through the broken glass, produced an eerie note. Apart from the general air of dismalness, the place was as I had left it the night before. Going up to the window, I examined the bars, closely; noting, as I did so, their comfortable thickness. Still, as I looked more intently, it seemed to me, that the middle bar was bent slightly from the straight; yet it was but trifling, and it might have been so for years. I had never, before, noticed them particularly.

"I put my hand through the broken window, and shook the bar. It was as firm as a rock. Perhaps the creatures had tried to 'start' it, and, finding it beyond their power, ceased from the effort. After that, I went round to each of the windows, in turn; examining them with careful attention; but nowhere else could I trace anything to show that there had been any tampering. Having finished my survey, I went back to the study, and poured myself out a little brandy. Then to the tower to watch.

Chapter VIII
After the Attack

I t was now about three a.m., and, presently, the Eastern sky began to pale with the coming of dawn. Gradually, the day came, and, by its light, I scanned the gardens, earnestly; but nowhere could I see any signs of the brutes. I leant over, and glanced down to the foot of the wall, to see whether the body of the Thing I had shot the night before was still there. It was gone. I supposed that others of the monsters had removed it during the night.

"Then, I went down on to the roof, and crossed over to the gap from which the copingstone had fallen. Reaching it, I looked over. Yes, there was the stone, as I had seen it last; but there was no appearance of anything beneath it; nor could I see the creatures I had killed, after its fall. Evidently, they also had been taken away. I turned, and went down to my study. There, I sat down, wearily. I was thoroughly tired. It was quite light now; though the sun's rays were not, as yet, perceptibly hot. A clock chimed the hour of four.

"I awoke, with a start, and looked round, hurriedly. The clock in the corner, indicated that it was three o'clock. It was already afternoon. I must have slept for nearly eleven hours.

"With a jerky movement, I sat forward in the chair, and listened. The house was perfectly silent. Slowly, I stood up, and yawned. I felt desperately tired, still, and sat down again; wondering what it was that had waked me.

"It must have been the clock striking, I concluded, presently; and was commencing to doze off, when a sudden noise brought me back, once more, to life. It was the sound of a step, as of a person moving cautiously down the corridor, towards my study. In an instant, I was on my feet, and grasping my rifle. Noiselessly, I waited. Had the creatures broken in, whilst I slept? Even as I questioned, the steps reached my door, halted momentarily, and then continued down the passage. Silently, I tiptoed to the doorway, and peeped out. Then, I experienced such a feeling of relief, as must a reprieved criminal—it was my sister. She was going towards the stairs.

"I stepped into the hall, and was about to call to her, when it occurred to me, that it was very queer she should have crept past my door, in that stealthy manner. I was puzzled, and, for one brief moment, the thought occupied my mind, that it was not she, but some fresh mystery of the house. Then, as I caught a glimpse of her old petticoat, the thought passed as quickly as it had come, and I half laughed. There could be no mistaking that ancient garment. Yet, I wondered what she was doing; and, remembering her condition of mind, on the previous day, I felt that it might be best to follow, quietly—taking care not to alarm her—and see what she was going to do. If she behaved rationally, well and good; if not, I should have to take steps to restrain her. I could run no unnecessary risks, under the danger that threatened us.

"Quickly, I reached the head of the stairs, and paused a moment. Then, I heard a sound that sent me leaping down, at a mad rate—it was the rattle of bolts being unshot. That foolish sister of mine was actually unbarring the back door.

"Just as her hand was on the last bolt, I reached her. She had not seen me, and, the first thing she knew, I had hold of her arm. She glanced up quickly, like a frightened animal, and screamed aloud.

" 'Come, Mary!' I said, sternly, 'what's the meaning of this nonsense? Do you mean to tell me you don't understand the danger, that you try to throw our two lives away in this fashion!'

"To this, she replied nothing; only trembled, violently, gasping and sobbing, as though in the last extremity of fear.

"Through some minutes, I reasoned with her; pointing out the need for caution, and asking her to be brave. There was little to be afraid of now, I explained—and, I tried to believe that I spoke the truth—but she must be sensible, and not attempt to leave the house for a few days.

"At last, I ceased, in despair. It was no use talking to her; she was, obviously, not quite herself for the time being. Finally, I told her she had better go to her room, if she could not behave rationally.

"Still, she took not any notice. So, without more ado, I picked her up in my arms, and carried her there. At first, she screamed, wildly; but had relapsed into silent trembling, by the time I reached the stairs.

"Arriving at her room, I laid her upon the bed. She lay there quietly enough, neither speaking nor sobbing—just shaking in a very ague of fear. I took a rug from a chair near by, and spread it over her. I could do nothing more for her, and so, crossed to where Pepper lay in a big basket. My sister had taken charge of him since his wound, to nurse him, for it had proved more severe than I had thought, and I was pleased to note that, in spite of her state of mind, she had looked after the old dog, carefully. Stooping, I spoke to him, and, in reply, he licked my hand, feebly. He was too ill to do more.

"Then, going to the bed, I bent over my sister, and asked her how she felt; but she only shook the more, and, much as it pained me, I had to admit that my presence seemed to make her worse.

"And so, I left her—locking the door, and pocketing the key. It seemed to be the only course to take.

"The rest of the day, I spent between the tower and my study. For food, I brought up a loaf from the pantry, and on this, and some claret, I lived for that day.

"What a long, weary day it was. If only I could have gone out into the gardens, as is my wont, I should have been content enough; but to be cooped in this silent house, with no companion, save a mad woman and a sick dog, was enough to prey upon the nerves of the hardiest. And out in the tangled shrubberies that surrounded the house, lurked—for all I could tell—those infernal Swine-creatures waiting their chance. Was ever a man in such straits?

"Once, in the afternoon, and again, later, I went to visit my sister. The second time, I found her tending Pepper; but, at my approach, she slid over, unobtrusively, to the far corner, with a gesture that saddened me beyond belief. Poor girl! her fear cut me intolerably, and I would not intrude on her, unnecessarily. She would be better, I trusted, in a few days; meanwhile, I could do nothing; and I judged it still needful—hard as it seemed—to keep her confined to her room. One thing there was that I took for encouragement: she had eaten some of the food I had taken to her, on my first visit.

"And so the day passed.

"As the evening drew on, the air grew chilly, and I began to make preparations for passing a second night in the tower—taking up two additional rifles, and a heavy ulster. The rifles I loaded, and laid alongside my other; as I intended to make things warm for any of the creatures who might show, during the night. I had plenty of ammunition, and I thought to give the brutes such a lesson, as should show them the uselessness of attempting to force an entrance.

"After that, I made the round of the house again; paying particular attention to the props that supported the study door. Then, feeling that I had done all that lay in my power to insure our safety, I returned to the tower; calling in on my sister and Pepper, for a final visit, on the way. Pepper was asleep; but woke, as I entered, and wagged his tail, in recognition. I thought he seemed slightly better. My sister was lying on the bed; though whether asleep or not, I was unable to tell; and thus I left them.

"Reaching the tower, I made myself as comfortable as circumstances would permit, and settled down to watch through the night. Gradually, darkness fell, and soon the details of the gardens were merged into shadows. During the first few hours, I sat, alert, listening for any sound that might help to tell me if anything were stirring down below. It was far too dark for my eyes to be of much use.

"Slowly, the hours passed; without anything unusual happening. And the moon rose, showing the gardens, apparently empty, and silent. And so, through the night, without disturbance or sound.

"Towards morning, I began to grow stiff and cold, with my long vigil; also, I was getting very uneasy, concerning the continued quietness on the part of the creatures. I mistrusted it, and would sooner, far, have had them attack the house, openly. Then, at least, I should have known my danger, and been able to meet it; but to wait like this, through a whole night, picturing all kinds of unknown devilment, was to jeopardise one's sanity. Once or twice, the thought came to me, that, perhaps, they had gone; but, in my heart, I found it impossible to believe that it was so.

Chapter IX

In the Cellars

"At last, what with being tired and cold, and the uneasiness that possessed me, I resolved to take a walk through the house; first calling in at the study, for a glass of brandy to warm me. This, I did, and, while there, I examined the door, carefully; but found all as I had left it the night before.

"The day was just breaking, as I left the tower; though it was still too dark in the house to be able to see without a light, and I took one of the study candles with me on my round. By the time I had finished the ground floor, the daylight was creeping in, wanly, through the barred windows. My search had shown me nothing fresh. Everything appeared to be in order, and I was on the point of extinguishing my candle, when the thought suggested itself to me to have another glance round the cellars. I had not, if I remember rightly, been into them since my hasty search on the evening of the attack.

"For, perhaps, the half of a minute, I hesitated. I would have been very willing to forego the task—as, indeed, I am inclined to think any man well might—for of all the great, awe-inspiring rooms in this house, the cellars are the hugest and weirdest. Great, gloomy caverns of places, unlit by any ray of daylight. Yet, I would not shirk the work. I felt that to do so would smack of sheer cowardice. Besides, as I reas-

sured myself, the cellars were really the most unlikely places in which to come across anything dangerous; considering that they can be entered, only through a heavy oaken door, the key of which, I carry always on my person.

"It is in the smallest of these places that I keep my wine; a gloomy hole close to the foot of the cellar stairs; and beyond which, I have seldom proceeded. Indeed, save for the rummage round, already mentioned, I doubt whether I had ever, before, been right through the cellars.

"As I unlocked the great door, at the top of the steps, I paused, nervously, a moment, at the strange, desolate smell that assailed my nostrils. Then, throwing the barrel of my weapon forward, I descended, slowly, into the darkness of the underground regions.

"Reaching the bottom of the stairs, I stood for a minute, and listened. All was silent, save for a faint drip, drip of water, falling, drop-by-drop, somewhere to my left. As I stood, I noticed how quietly the candle burnt; never a flicker nor flare, so utterly windless was the place.

"Quietly, I moved from cellar to cellar. I had but a very dim memory of their arrangement. The impressions left by my first search were blurred. I had recollections of a succession of great cellars, and of one, greater than the rest, the roof of which was upheld by pillars; beyond that my mind was hazy, and predominated by a sense of cold and darkness and shadows. Now, however, it was different; for, although nervous, I was sufficiently collected to be able to look about me, and note the structure and size of the different vaults I entered.

"Of course, with the amount of light given by my candle, it was not possible to examine each place, minutely, but I was enabled to notice, as I went along, that the walls appeared to be built with wonderful precision and finish; while here and there, an occasional, massive pillar shot up to support the vaulted roof.

"Thus, I came, at last, to the great cellar that I remembered. It is reached, through a huge, arched entrance, on which I observed strange, fantastic carvings, which threw queer shadows under the light of my candle. As I stood, and examined these, thoughtfully, it occurred to me how strange it was, that I should be so little acquainted with my own house. Yet, this may be easily understood, when one realises the size of this ancient pile, and the fact that only my old sister and I live in it, occupying a few of the rooms, such as our wants decide.

"Holding the light high, I passed on into the cellar, and, keeping to the right, paced slowly up, until I reached the further end. I walked quietly, and looked cautiously about, as I went. But, so far as the light showed, I saw nothing unusual.

"At the top, I turned to the left, still keeping to the wall, and so continued, until I had traversed the whole of the vast chamber. As I moved along, I noticed that the floor was composed of solid rock, in places covered with a damp mould, in others bare, or almost so, save for a thin coating of light-grey dust.

"I had halted at the doorway. Now, however, I turned, and made my way up the centre of the place; passing among the pillars, and glancing to right and left, as I moved. About halfway up the cellar, I stubbed my foot against something that gave out a metallic sound. Stooping quickly, I held the candle, and saw that the object I had kicked, was a large, metal ring. Bending lower, I cleared the dust from around it, and, presently, discovered that it was attached to a ponderous trap door, black with age.

"Feeling excited, and wondering to where it could lead, I laid my gun on the floor, and, sticking the candle in the trigger guard, took the ring in both hands, and pulled. The trap creaked loudly—the sound echoing, vaguely, through the huge place—and opened, heavily.

"Propping the edge on my knee, I reached for the candle, and held it in the opening, moving it to right and left; but could see nothing. I was puzzled and surprised. There were no signs of steps, nor even the appearance of there ever having been any. Nothing; save an empty blackness. I might have been looking down into a bottomless, sideless well. Then, even as I stared, full of perplexity, I seemed to hear, far down, as though from untold depths, a faint whisper of sound. I bent my head, quickly, more into the opening, and listened, intently. It may have been fancy; but I could have sworn to hearing a soft titter, that grew into a hideous, chuckling, faint and distant. Startled, I leapt backwards, letting the trap fall, with a hollow clang, that filled the place with echoes. Even then, I seemed to hear that mocking, suggestive laughter; but this, I knew, must be my imagination. The sound, I had heard, was far too slight to penetrate through the cumbrous trap.

"For a full minute, I stood there, quivering—glancing, nervously, behind and before; but the great cellar was silent as a grave, and, gradually, I shook off the frightened sensation. With a calmer mind, I became again curious to know into what that trap opened; but could not, then, summon sufficient courage to make a further investigation. One thing I felt, however, was that the trap ought to be secured. This, I accomplished by placing upon it several large pieces of 'dressed' stone, which I had noticed in my tour along the East wall.

"Then, after a final scrutiny of the rest of the place, I retraced my way through the cellars, to the stairs, and so reached the daylight, with an infinite feeling of relief, that the uncomfortable task was accomplished.

Chapter X
The Time of Waiting

"The sun was now warm, and shining brightly, forming a wondrous contrast to the dark and dismal cellars; and it was with comparatively light feelings, that I made my way up to the tower, to survey the gardens. There, I found everything quiet, and, after a few minutes, went down to Mary's room.

"Here, having knocked, and received a reply, I unlocked the door. My sister was sitting, quietly, on the bed; as though waiting. She seemed quite herself again, and made no attempt to move away, as I approached; yet, I observed that she scanned my face, anxiously, as though in doubt, and but half assured in her mind that there was nothing to fear from me.

"To my questions, as to how she felt, she replied, sanely enough, that she was hungry, and would like to go down to prepare breakfast, if I did not mind. For a minute, I meditated whether it would be safe to let her out. Finally, I told her she might go, on condition that she promised not to attempt to leave the house, or meddle with any of the outer doors. At my mention of the doors, a sudden look of fright crossed her face; but she said nothing, save to give the required promise, and then left the room, silently.

"Crossing the floor, I approached Pepper. He had waked as I entered; but, beyond a slight yelp of pleasure, and a soft rapping with his tail, had kept quiet. Now, as I patted him, he made an attempt to stand up, and succeeded, only to fall back on his side, with a little yowl of pain.

"I spoke to him, and bade him lie still. I was greatly delighted with his improvement, and also with the natural kindness of my sister's heart, in taking such good care of him, in spite of her condition of mind. After a while, I left him, and went downstairs, to my study.

"In a little time, Mary appeared, carrying a tray on which smoked a hot breakfast. As she entered the room, I saw her gaze fasten on the props that supported the study door; her lips tightened, and I thought she paled, slightly; but that was all. Putting the tray down at my elbow, she was leaving the room, quietly, when I called her back. She came, it seemed, a little timidly, as though startled; and I noted that her hand clutched at her apron, nervously.

" 'Come, Mary,' I said. 'Cheer up! Things look brighter. I've seen none of the creatures since yesterday morning, early.'

"She looked at me, in a curiously puzzled manner; as though not comprehending. Then, intelligence swept into her eyes, and fear; but she said nothing, beyond an unintelligible murmur of acquiescence. After that, I kept silence; it was evident that any reference to the Swine-things, was more than her shaken nerves could bear.

"Breakfast over, I went up to the tower. Here, during the greater part of the day, I maintained a strict watch over the gardens. Once or twice, I went down to the basement, to see how my sister was getting along. Each time, I found her quiet, and curiously submissive. Indeed, on the last occasion, she even ventured to address me, on her own account, with regard to some household matter that needed attention. Though this was done with an almost extraordinary timidity, I hailed it with happiness, as being the first word, voluntarily spoken, since the critical moment, when

I had caught her unbarring the back door, to go out among those waiting brutes. I wondered whether she was aware of her attempt, and how near a thing it had been; but refrained from questioning her, thinking it best to let well alone.

"That night, I slept in a bed; the first time for two nights. In the morning, I rose early, and took a walk through the house. All was as it should be, and I went up to the tower, to have a look at the gardens. Here, again, I found perfect quietness.

"At breakfast, when I met Mary, I was greatly pleased to see that she had sufficiently regained command over herself, to be able to greet me in a perfectly natural manner. She talked sensibly and quietly; only keeping carefully from any mention of the past couple of days. In this, I humoured her, to the extent of not attempting to lead the conversation in that direction.

"Earlier in the morning, I had been to see Pepper. He was mending, rapidly; and bade fair to be on his legs, in earnest, in another day or two. Before leaving the breakfast table, I made some reference to his improvement. In the short discussion that followed, I was surprised to gather, from my sister's remarks, that she was still under the impression that his wound had been given by the wildcat, of my invention. It made me feel almost ashamed of myself for deceiving her. Yet, the lie had been told to prevent her from being frightened. And then, I had been sure that she must have known the truth, later, when those brutes had attacked the house.

"During the day, I kept on the alert; spending much of my time, as on the previous day, in the tower; but not a sign could I see of the Swine-creatures, nor hear any sound. Several times, the thought had come to me, that the Things had, at last, left us; but, up to this time, I had refused to entertain the idea, seriously; now, however, I began to feel that there was reason for hope. It would soon be three days since I had seen any of the Things; but still, I intended to use the utmost caution. For all that I could tell, this protracted silence might be a ruse to tempt me from the house—perhaps right into their arms. The thought of such a contingency, was, alone, sufficient to make me circumspect.

"So it was, that the fourth, fifth and sixth days went by, quietly, without my making any attempt to leave the house.

"On the sixth day, I had the pleasure of seeing Pepper, once more, upon his feet; and, though still very weak, he managed to keep me company during the whole of that day.

Chapter XI
The Searching of the Gardens

"How slowly the time went; and never a thing to indicate that any of the brutes still infested the gardens.

"It was on the ninth day that, finally, I decided to run the risk, if any there were, and sally out. With this purpose in view, I loaded one of the shotguns, carefully—choosing it, as being more deadly than a rifle, at close quarters; and then, after a final scrutiny of the grounds, from the tower, I called Pepper to follow me, and made my way down to the basement.

"At the door, I must confess to hesitating a moment. The thought of what might be awaiting me among the dark shrubberies, was by no means calculated to encourage my resolution. It was but a second, though, and then I had drawn the bolts, and was standing on the path outside the door.

"Pepper followed, stopping at the doorstep to sniff, suspiciously; and carrying his nose up and down the jambs, as though following a scent. Then, suddenly, he turned, sharply, and started to run here and there, in semicircles and circles, all around the door; finally returning to the threshold. Here, he began again to nose about.

"Hitherto, I had stood, watching the dog; yet, all the time, with half my gaze on the wild tangle of gardens, stretching round me. Now, I went towards him, and, bending down, examined the surface of the door, where he was smelling. I found that the wood was covered with a network of scratches, crossing and recrossing one another, in inextricable confusion. In addition to this, I noticed that the doorposts, themselves, were gnawed in places. Beyond these, I could find nothing; and so, standing up, I began to make the tour of the house wall.

"Pepper, as soon as I walked away, left the door, and ran ahead, still nosing and sniffing as he went along. At times, he stopped to investigate. Here, it would be a bullet-hole in the pathway, or, perhaps, a powder stained wad. Anon, it might be a piece of torn sod, or a disturbed patch of weedy path; but, save for such trifles, he found nothing. I observed him, critically, as he went along, and could discover nothing of uneasiness, in his demeanour, to indicate that he felt the nearness of any of the creatures. By this, I was assured that the gardens were empty, at least for the present, of those hateful Things. Pepper could not be easily deceived, and it was a relief to feel that he would know, and give me timely warning, if there were any danger.

"Reaching the place where I had shot that first creature, I stopped, and made a careful scrutiny; but could see nothing. From there, I went on to where the great copingstone had fallen. It lay on its side, apparently just as it had been left when I shot the brute that was moving it. A couple of feet to the right of the nearer end, was a great dent in the ground; showing where it had struck. The other end was still within the indentation—half in, and half out. Going nearer, I looked at the stone, more closely. What a huge piece of masonry it was! And that creature had moved it, single-handed, in its attempt to reach what lay below.

"I went round to the further end of the stone. Here, I found that it was possible to see under it, for a distance of nearly a couple of feet. Still, I could see nothing of the stricken creatures, and I felt much surprised. I had, as I have before said, guessed that the remains had been removed; yet, I could not conceive that it had been done so thoroughly as not to leave some certain sign, beneath the stone, indicative of their fate. I had seen several of the brutes struck down beneath it, with such force that they must have been literally driven into the earth; and now, not a vestige of them was to be seen—not even a bloodstain.

"I felt more puzzled, than ever, as I turned the matter over in my mind; but could think of no plausible explanation; and so, finally, gave it up, as one of the many things that were unexplainable.

"From there, I transferred my attention to the study door. I could see, now, even more plainly, the effects of the tremendous strain, to which it had been subjected; and I marvelled how, even with the support afforded by the props, it had withstood the attacks, so well. There were no marks of blows—indeed, none had been given—but the door had been literally riven from its hinges, by the application of enormous, silent force. One thing that I observed affected me profoundly—the head of one of the props had been driven right through a panel. This was, of itself, sufficient to show how huge an effort the creatures had made to break down the door, and how nearly they had succeeded.

"Leaving, I continued my tour round the house, finding little else of interest; save at the back, where I came across the piece of piping I had torn from the wall, lying among the long grass underneath the broken window.

"Then, I returned to the house, and, having re-bolted the back door, went up to the tower. Here, I spent the afternoon, reading, and occasionally glancing down into the gardens. I had determined, if the night passed quietly, to go as far as the Pit, on the morrow. Perhaps, I should be able to learn, then, something of what had happened. The day slipped away, and the night came, and went much as the last few nights had gone.

"When I rose the morning had broken, fine and clear; and I determined to put my project into action. During breakfast, I considered the matter, carefully; after which, I went to the study for my shotgun. In addition, I loaded, and slipped into my pocket, a small, but heavy, pistol. I quite understood that, if there were any danger, it lay in the direction of the Pit and I intended to be prepared.

"Leaving the study, I went down to the back door, followed by Pepper. Once outside, I took a quick survey of the surrounding gardens, and then set off towards the Pit. On the way, I kept a sharp outlook, holding my gun, handily. Pepper was running ahead, I noticed, without any apparent hesitation. From this, I augured that there was no imminent danger to be apprehended, and I stepped out more quickly in his wake. He had reached the top of the Pit, now, and was nosing his way along the edge.

"A minute later, I was beside him, looking down into the Pit. For a moment, I could scarcely believe that it was the same place, so greatly was it changed. The dark, wooded ravine of a fortnight ago, with a foliage-hidden stream, running sluggishly, at the bottom, existed no longer. Instead, my eyes showed me a ragged chasm, partly filled with a gloomy lake of turbid water. All one side of the ravine was stripped of underwood, showing the bare rock.

"A little to my left, the side of the Pit appeared to have collapsed altogether, forming a deep V-shaped cleft in the face of the rocky cliff. This rift ran, from the upper edge of the ravine, nearly down to the water, and penetrated into the Pit side, to a distance of some forty feet. Its opening was, at least, six yards across; and, from this, it seemed to taper into about two. But, what attracted my attention, more than even the stupendous split itself, was a great hole,

some distance down the cleft, and right in the angle of the V. It was clearly defined, and not unlike an arched doorway in shape; though, lying as it did in the shadow, I could not see it very distinctly.

"The opposite side of the Pit, still retained its verdure; but so torn in places, and everywhere covered with dust and rubbish, that it was hardly distinguishable as such.

"My first impression, that there had been a land slip, was, I began to see, not sufficient, of itself, to account for all the changes I witnessed. And the water—? I turned, suddenly; for I had become aware that, somewhere to my right, there was a noise of running water. I could see nothing; but, now that my attention had been caught, I distinguished, easily, that it came from somewhere at the East end of the Pit.

"Slowly, I made my way in that direction; the sound growing plainer as I advanced, until in a little, I stood right above it. Even then, I could not perceive the cause, until I knelt down, and thrust my head over the cliff. Here, the noise came up to me, plainly; and I saw, below me, a torrent of clear water, issuing from a small fissure in the Pit side, and rushing down the rocks, into the lake beneath. A little further along the cliff, I saw another, and, beyond that again, two smaller ones. These, then, would help to account for the quantity of water in the Pit; and, if the fall of rock and earth had blocked the outlet of the stream at the bottom, there was little doubt but that it was contributing a very large share.

"Yet, I puzzled my head to account for the general-ly *shaken* appearance of the place—these streamlets, and that huge cleft, further up the ravine! It seemed to me, that more than the landslip was necessary to account for these. I could imagine an earthquake, or a great *explosion*, creating some such condition of affairs as existed; but, of these, there had been neither. Then, I stood up, quickly, remembering that crash, and the cloud of dust that had followed, directly, rushing high into the air. But I shook my head, unbelievingly. No! It must have been the noise of the falling rocks and earth, I had heard; of course, the dust would fly, naturally. Still, in spite of my reasoning, I had an uneasy feeling, that this theory did not satisfy my sense of the probable; and yet, was any other, that I could suggest, likely to be half so plausible? Pepper had been sitting on the grass, while I conducted my examination. Now, as I turned up the North side of the ravine, he rose and followed.

"Slowly, and keeping a careful watch in all directions, I made the circuit of the Pit; but found little else, that I had not already seen. From the West end, I could see the four waterfalls, uninterruptedly. They were some considerable distance up from the surface of the lake—about fifty feet, I calculated.

"For a little while longer, I loitered about; keeping my eyes and ears open, but still, without seeing or hearing anything suspicious. The whole place was wonderfully quiet; indeed, save for the continuous murmur of the water, at the top end, no sound, of any description, broke the silence.

"All this while, Pepper had shown no signs of uneasiness. This seemed, to me, to indicate that, for the time being, at least, there was none of the Swine-creatures in the vicinity. So far as I could see, his attention appeared to have been taken, chiefly, with scratching and sniffing among the grass at the edge of the Pit. At times, he would leave the edge, and run along towards the house, as though following invisible tracks; but, in all cases, returning after a few minutes. I had little doubt but that he was really tracing out the footsteps of the Swine-things; and the very fact that each one seemed to lead him back to the Pit, appeared to me, a proof that the brutes had all returned whence they came.

"At noon, I went home, for dinner. During the afternoon, I made a partial search of the gardens, accompanied by Pepper; but, without coming upon anything to indicate the presence of the creatures.

"Once, as we made our way through the shrubberies, Pepper rushed in among some bushes, with a fierce yelp. At that, I jumped back, in sudden fright, and threw my gun forward, in readiness; only to laugh, nervously, as Pepper reappeared, chasing an unfortunate cat. Towards evening, I gave up the search, and returned to the house. All at once, as we were passing a great clump of bushes, on our right, Pepper disappeared, and I could hear him sniffing and growling among them, in a suspicious manner. With my gun barrel, I parted the intervening shrubbery, and looked inside. There was nothing to be seen, save that many of the branches were bent down, and broken; as though some animal had made a lair there, at no very previous date. It was probably, I thought, one of the places occupied by some of the Swine-creatures, on the night of the attack.

"Next day, I resumed my search through the gardens; but without result. By evening, I had been right through them, and now, I knew, beyond the possibility of doubt, that there were no longer any of the Things concealed about the place. Indeed, I have often thought since, that I was correct in my earlier surmise, that they had left soon after the attack.

Chapter XII

The Subterranean Pit

"Another week came and went, during which I spent a great deal of my time about the Pit mouth. I had come to the conclusion a few days earlier, that the arched hole, in the angle of the great rift, was the place through which the Swine-things had made their exit, from some unholy place in the bowels of the world. How near the probable truth this went, I was to learn later.

"It may be easily understood, that I was tremendously curious, though in a frightened way, to know to what infernal place that hole led; though, so far, the idea had not struck me, seriously, of making an investigation. I was far too much imbued with a sense of horror of the Swine-creatures, to think of venturing, willingly, where there was any chance of coming into contact with them.

"Gradually, however, as time passed, this feeling grew insensibly less; so that when, a few days later, the thought occurred to me that it might be possible to clamber down and have a look into the hole, I was not so exceedingly averse to it, as might have been imagined. Still, I do not think, even then, that I really intended to try any such foolhardy adventure. For all that I could tell, it might be certain death, to enter that doleful looking opening. And yet, such is the pertinacity of human curiosity, that, at last, my chief desire was but to discover what lay beyond that gloomy entrance.

"Slowly, as the days slid by, my fear of the Swine-things became an emotion of the past—more an unpleasant, incredible memory, than aught else.

"Thus, a day came, when, throwing thoughts and fancies adrift, I procured a rope from the house, and, having made it fast to a stout tree, at the top of the rift, and some little distance back from the Pit edge, let the other end down into the cleft, until it dangled right across the mouth of the dark hole.

"Then, cautiously, and with many misgivings as to whether it was not a mad act that I was attempting, I climbed slowly down, using the rope as a support, until I reached the hole. Here, still holding on to the rope, I stood, and peered in. All was perfectly dark, and not a sound came to me. Yet, a moment later, it seemed that I could hear something. I held my breath, and listened; but all was silent as the grave, and I breathed freely once more. At the same instant, I heard the sound again. It was like a noise of laboured breathing—deep and sharp-drawn. For a short second, I stood, petrified; not able to move. But now the sounds had ceased again, and I could hear nothing.

"As I stood there, anxiously, my foot dislodged a pebble, which fell inward, into the dark, with a hollow chink. At once, the noise was taken up and repeated a score of times; each succeeding echo being fainter, and seeming to travel away from me, as though into remote distance. Then, as the silence fell again, I heard that stealthy breathing. For each respiration I made, I could hear an answering breath. The sounds appeared to be coming nearer; and then, I heard several others; but fainter and more distant. Why I did not grip the rope, and spring up out of danger, I cannot say. It was as though I had been paralysed. I broke out into a profuse sweat, and tried to moisten my lips with my tongue. My throat had gone suddenly dry, and I coughed, huskily. It came back to me, in a dozen, horrible, throaty tones, mockingly. I peered, helplessly, into the gloom; but still nothing showed. I had a strange, choky sensation, and again I coughed, dryly. Again the echo took it up, rising and falling, grotesquely, and dying slowly into a muffled silence.

"Then, suddenly, a thought came to me, and I held my breath. The other breathing stopped. I breathed again, and, once more, it re-commenced. But now, I no longer feared. I knew that the strange sounds were not made by any lurking Swine-creature; but were simply the echo of my own respirations.

"Yet, I had received such a fright, that I was glad to scramble up the rift, and haul up the rope. I was far too shaken and nervous to think of entering that dark hole then, and so returned to the house. I felt more myself next morning; but even then, I could not summon up sufficient courage to explore the place.

"All this time, the water in the Pit had been creeping slowly up, and now stood but a little below the opening. At the rate at which it was rising, it would be level with the floor in less than another week; and I realised that, unless I carried out my investigations soon, I should probably never do so at all; as the water would rise and rise, until the opening, itself, was submerged.

"It may have been that this thought stirred me to act; but, whatever it was, a couple of days later, saw me standing at the top of the cleft, fully equipped for the task.

"This time, I was resolved to conquer my shirking, and go right through with the matter. With this intention, I had brought, in addition to the rope, a bundle of candles, meaning to use them as a torch; also my double-barrelled shotgun. In my belt, I had a heavy horse-pistol, loaded with buckshot.

"As before, I fastened the rope to the tree. Then, having tied my gun across my shoulders, with a piece of stout cord,

I lowered myself over the edge of the Pit. At this movement, Pepper, who had been eyeing my actions, watchfully, rose to his feet, and ran to me, with a half bark, half wail, it seemed to me, of warning. But I was resolved on my enterprise, and bade him lie down. I would much have liked to take him with me; but this was next to impossible, in the existing circumstances. As my face dropped level with the Pit edge, he licked me, right across the mouth; and then, seizing my sleeve between his teeth, began to pull back, strongly. It was very evident that he did not want me to go. Yet, having made up my mind, I had no intention of giving up the attempt; and, with a sharp word to Pepper, to release me, I continued my descent, leaving the poor old fellow at the top, barking and crying like a forsaken pup.

"Carefully, I lowered myself from projection to projection. I knew that a slip might mean a wetting.

"Reaching the entrance, I let go the rope, and untied the gun from my shoulders. Then, with a last look at the sky—which I noticed was clouding over, rapidly—I went forward a couple of paces, so as to be shielded from the wind, and lit one of the candles. Holding it above my head, and grasping my gun, firmly, I began to move on, slowly, throwing my glances in all directions.

"For the first minute, I could hear the melancholy sound of Pepper's howling, coming down to me. Gradually, as I penetrated further into the darkness, it grew fainter; until, in a little while, I could hear nothing. The path tended downward somewhat, and to the left. Thence it kept on, still running to the left, until I found that it was leading me right in the direction of the house.

"Very cautiously, I moved onward, stopping, every few steps, to listen. I had gone, perhaps, a hundred yards, when, suddenly, it seemed to me that I caught a faint sound, somewhere along the passage behind. With my heart thudding heavily, I listened. The noise grew plainer, and appeared to be approaching, rapidly. I could hear it distinctly, now. It was the soft padding of running feet. In the first moments of fright, I stood, irresolute; not knowing whether to go forward or backward. Then, with a sudden realization of the best thing to do, I backed up to the rocky wall on my right, and, holding the candle above my head, waited—gun in hand—cursing my foolhardy curiosity, for bringing me into such a strait.

"I had not long to wait, but a few seconds, before two eyes reflected back from the gloom, the rays of my candle. I raised my gun, using my right hand only, and aimed quickly. Even as I did so, something leapt out of the darkness, with a blustering bark of joy that woke the echoes, like thunder. It was Pepper. How he had contrived to scramble down the cleft, I could not conceive. As I brushed my hand, nervously, over his coat, I noticed that he was dripping; and concluded that he must have tried to follow me, and fallen into the water; from which he would not find it very difficult to climb.

"Having waited a minute, or so, to steady myself, I proceeded along the way, Pepper following, quietly. I was curiously glad to have the old fellow with me. He was company, and, somehow, with him at my heels, I was less afraid. Also, I knew how quickly his keen ears would detect the presence of any unwelcome creature, should there be such, amid the darkness that wrapped us.

"For some minutes we went slowly along; the path still leading straight towards the house. Soon, I concluded, we should be standing right beneath it, did the path but carry far enough. I led the way, cautiously, for another fifty yards, or so. Then, I stopped, and held the light high; and reason enough I had to be thankful that I did so; for there, not three paces forward, the path vanished, and, in place, showed a hollow blackness, that sent sudden fear through me.

"Very cautiously, I crept forward, and peered down; but could see nothing. Then, I crossed to the left of the passage, to see whether there might be any continuation of the path. Here, right against the wall, I found that a narrow track, some three feet wide, led onward. Carefully, I stepped on to it; but had not gone far, before I regretted venturing thereon. For, after a few paces, the already narrow way, resolved itself into a mere ledge, with, on the one side the solid, unyielding rock, towering up, in a great wall, to the unseen roof, and, on the other, that yawning chasm. I could not help reflecting how helpless I was, should I be attacked there, with no room to turn, and where even the recoil of my weapon might be sufficient to drive me headlong into the depths below.

"To my great relief, a little further on, the track suddenly broadened out again to its original breadth. Gradually, as I went onward, I noticed that the path trended steadily to the right, and so, after some minutes, I discovered that I was not going forward; but simply circling the huge abyss. I had, evidently, come to the end of the great passage.

"Five minutes later, I stood on the spot from which I had started; having been completely round, what I guessed now to be a vast pit, the mouth of which must be at least a hundred yards across.

"For some little time, I stood there, lost in perplexing thought. 'What does it all mean?' was the cry that had begun to reiterate through my brain.

"A sudden idea struck me, and I searched round for a piece of stone. Presently, I found a bit of rock, about the size of a small loaf. Sticking the candle upright in a crevice of the floor, I went back from the edge, somewhat, and, taking a short run, launched the stone forward into the chasm—my idea being to throw it far enough to keep it clear of the sides. Then, I stooped forward, and listened;

but, though I kept perfectly quiet, for at least a full minute, no sound came back to me from out of the dark.

"I knew, then, that the depth of the hole must be immense; for the stone, had it struck anything, was large enough to have set the echoes of that weird place, whispering for an indefinite period. Even as it was, the cavern had given back the sounds of my footfalls, multitudinously. The place was awesome, and I would willingly have retraced my steps, and left the mysteries of its solitudes unsolved; only, to do so, meant admitting defeat.

"Then, a thought came, to try to get a view of the abyss. It occurred to me that, if I placed my candles round the edge of the hole, I should be able to get, at least, some dim sight of the place.

I found, on counting, that I had brought fifteen candles, in the bundle—my first intention having been, as I have already said, to make a torch of the lot. These, I proceeded to place round the Pit mouth, with an interval of about twenty yards between each.

"Having completed the circle, I stood in the passage, and endeavoured to get an idea of how the place looked. But I discovered, immediately, that they were totally insufficient for my purpose. They did little more than make the gloom visible. One thing they did, however, and that was, they confirmed my opinion of the size of the opening; and, although they showed me nothing that I wanted to see; yet the contrast they afforded to the heavy darkness, pleased me, curiously. It was as though fifteen tiny stars shone through the subterranean night.

"Then, even as I stood, Pepper gave a sudden howl, that was taken up by the echoes, and repeated with ghastly variations, dying away, slowly. With a quick movement, I held aloft the one candle that I had kept, and glanced down at the dog; at the same moment, I seemed to hear a noise, like a diabolical chuckle, rise up from the hitherto, silent depths of the Pit. I started; then, I recollected that it was, probably, the echo of Pepper's howl.

"Pepper had moved away from me, up the passage, a few steps; he was nosing along the rocky floor; and I thought I heard him lapping. I went towards him, holding the candle low. As I moved, I heard my boot go sop, sop; and the light was reflected from something that glistened, and crept past my feet, swiftly towards the Pit. I bent lower, and looked; then gave vent to an expression of surprise. From somewhere, higher up the path, a stream of water was running quickly in the direction of the great opening, and growing in size every second.

"Again, Pepper gave vent to that deep-drawn howl, and, running at me, seized my coat, and attempted to drag me up the path towards the entrance. With a nervous gesture, I shook him off, and crossed quickly over to the left-hand wall. If anything were coming, I was going to have the wall at my back.

"Then, as I stared anxiously up the pathway, my candle caught a gleam, far up the passage. At the same moment, I became conscious of a murmurous roar, that grew louder, and filled the whole cavern with deafening sound. From the Pit, came a deep, hollow echo, like the sob of a giant. Then, I had sprung to one side, on to the narrow ledge that ran round the abyss, and, turning, saw a great wall of foam sweep past me, and leap tumultuously into the waiting chasm. A cloud of spray burst over me, extinguishing my candle, and wetting me to the skin. I still held my gun. The three nearest candles went out; but the further ones gave only a short flicker. After the first rush, the flow of water eased down to a steady stream, maybe a foot in depth; though I could not see this, until I had procured one of the lighted candles, and, with it, started to reconnoitre. Pepper had, fortunately, followed me as I leapt for the ledge, and now, very much subdued, kept close behind.

"A short examination showed me that the water reached right across the passage, and was running at a tremendous rate. Already, even as I stood there, it had deepened. I could make only a guess at what had happened. Evidently, the water in the ravine had broken into the passage, by some means. If that were the case, it would go on increasing in volume, until I should find it impossible to leave the place. The thought was frightening. It was evident that I must make my exit as hurriedly as possible.

"Taking my gun by the stock, I sounded the water. It was a little under knee-deep. The noise it made, plunging down into the Pit, was deafening. Then, with a call to Pepper, I stepped out into the flood, using the gun as a staff. Instantly, the water boiled up over my knees, and nearly to the tops of my thighs, with the speed at which it was racing. For one short moment, I nearly lost my footing; but the thought of what lay behind, stimulated me to a fierce endeavour, and, step-by-step, I made headway.

"Of Pepper, I knew nothing at first. I had all I could do to keep on my legs; and was overjoyed, when he appeared beside me. He was wading manfully along. He is a big dog, with longish thin legs, and I suppose the water had less grasp on them, than upon mine. Anyway, he managed a great deal better than I did; going ahead of me, like a guide, and wittingly—or otherwise—helping, somewhat, to break the force of the water. On we went, step by step, struggling and gasping, until somewhere about a hundred yards had been safely traversed. Then, whether it was because I was taking less care, or that there was a slippery place on the rocky floor, I cannot say; but, suddenly, I slipped, and fell on my face. Instantly, the water leapt over me in a cataract, hurling me down, towards that bottomless hole, at a frightful speed. Frantically I struggled; but it was impossible to get a footing. I was helpless, gasping and drowning. All at once, something gripped my coat, and brought me to a standstill. It was Pepper. Missing me, he must have raced back, through the dark turmoil, to find me, and then caught, and held me, until I was able to get to my feet.

"I have a dim recollection of having seen, momentarily, the gleams of several lights; but, of this, I have never been quite sure. If my impressions are correct, I must have been washed down to the very brink of that awful chasm, before Pepper managed to bring me to a standstill. And the lights, of course, could only have been the distant flames of the candles, I had left burning. But, as I have said, I am not by any means sure. My eyes were full of water, and I had been badly shaken.

"And there was I, without my helpful gun, without light, and sadly confused, with the water deepening; depending solely upon my old friend Pepper, to help me out of that hellish place.

"I was facing the torrent. Naturally, it was the only way in which I could have sustained my position a moment; for even old Pepper could not have held me long against that terrific strain, without assistance, however blind, from me.

"Perhaps a minute passed, during which it was touch and go with me; then, gradually I re-commenced my tortuous way up the passage. And so began the grimmest fight with death, from which ever I hope to emerge victorious. Slowly, furiously, almost hopelessly, I strove; and that faithful Pepper led me, dragged me, upward and onward, until, at last, ahead I saw a gleam of blessed light. It was the entrance. Only a few yards further, and I reached the opening, with the water surging and boiling hungrily around my loins.

"And now I understood the cause of the catastrophe. It was raining heavily, literally in torrents. The surface of the lake was level with the bottom of the opening—nay! more than level, it was above it. Evidently, the rain had swollen the lake, and caused this premature rise; for, at the rate the ravine had been filling, it would not have reached the entrance for a couple more days.

"Luckily, the rope by which I had descended, was streaming into the opening, upon the inrushing waters. Seizing the end, I knotted it securely round Pepper's body, then, summoning up the last remnant of my strength, I commenced to swarm up the side of the cliff. I reached the Pit edge, in the last stage of exhaustion. Yet, I had to make one more effort, and haul Pepper into safety.

"Slowly and wearily, I hauled on the rope. Once or twice, it seemed that I should have to give up; for Pepper is a weighty dog, and I was utterly done. Yet, to let go, would have meant certain death to the old fellow, and the thought spurred me to greater exertions. I have but a very hazy remembrance of the end. I recall pulling, through moments that lagged strangely. I have also some recollection of seeing Pepper's muzzle, appearing over the Pit edge, after what seemed an indefinite period of time. Then, all grew suddenly dark.

Chapter XIII
The Trap in the Great Cellar

"I suppose I must have swooned; for, the next thing I remember, I opened my eyes, and all was dusk. I was lying on my back, with one leg doubled under the other, and Pepper was licking my ears. I felt horribly stiff, and my leg was numb, from the knee, downwards. For a few minutes, I lay thus, in a dazed condition; then, slowly, I struggled to a sitting position, and looked about me.

It had stopped raining, but the trees still dripped, dismally. From the Pit, came a continuous murmur of running water. I felt cold and shivery. My clothes were sodden, and I ached all over. Very slowly, the life came back into my numbed leg, and, after a little, I essayed to stand up. This, I managed, at the second attempt; but I was very tottery, and peculiarly weak. It seemed to me, that I was going to be ill, and I made shift to stumble my way towards the house. My steps were erratic, and my head confused. At each step that I took, sharp pains shot through my limbs.

"I had gone, perhaps, some thirty paces, when a cry from Pepper, drew my attention, and I turned, stiffly, towards him. The old dog was trying to follow me; but could come no further, owing to the rope, with which I had hauled him up, being still tied round his body, the other end not having been unfastened from the tree. For a moment, I fumbled with the knots, weakly; but they were wet and hard, and I could do nothing. Then, I remembered my knife, and, in a minute, the rope was cut.

"How I reached the house, I scarcely know, and, of the days that followed, I remember still less. Of one thing, I am certain, that, had it not been for my sister's untiring love and nursing, I had not been writing at this moment.

"When I recovered my senses, it was to find that I had been in bed for nearly two weeks. Yet another week passed, before I was strong enough to totter out into the gardens. Even then, I was not able to walk so far as the Pit. I would have liked to ask my sister, how high the water had risen; but felt it was wiser not to mention the subject to her. Indeed, since then, I have made a rule never to speak to her about the strange things, that happen in this great, old house.

"It was not until a couple of days later, that I managed to get across to the Pit. There, I found that, in my few weeks' absence, there had been wrought a wondrous change. Instead of the three-parts filled ravine, I looked out upon a great lake, whose placid surface, reflected the light, coldly. The water had risen to within half a dozen feet of the Pit edge. Only in one part was the lake disturbed, and that was above the place where, far down under the silent waters, yawned the entrance to the vast, underground Pit. Here, there was a continuous bubbling; and, occasionally, a curious sort of sobbing gurgle would find its way up from the depth. Beyond these, there was nothing to tell of the things that were hidden beneath. As I stood there, it came to me how wonderfully things had worked out. The entrance to the place whence the Swine-creatures had come, was sealed up, by a power that made me feel there was nothing more to fear from them. And yet, with the feeling, there was a sensation that, now, I should never learn anything further, of the place from which those dreadful Things had come. It was completely shut off and concealed from human curiosity forever.

"Strange—in the knowledge of that underground hell-hole—how apposite has been the naming of the Pit. One wonders how it originated, and when. Naturally, one concludes that the shape and depth of the ravine would suggest the name 'Pit'. Yet, is it not possible that it has, all along, held a deeper significance, a hint—could one but have guessed—of the greater, more stupendous Pit that lies far down in the earth, beneath this old house? Under this house! Even now, the idea is strange and terrible to me. For I have proved, beyond doubt, that the Pit yawns right below the house, which is evidently supported, somewhere above the centre of it, upon a tremendous, arched roof, of solid rock.

"It happened in this wise, that, having occasion to go down to the cellars, the thought occurred to me to pay a visit to the great vault, where the trap is situated; and see whether everything was as I had left it.

"Reaching the place, I walked slowly up the centre, until I came to the trap. There it was, with the stones piled upon it, just as I had seen it last. I had a lantern with me, and the idea came to me, that now would be a good time to investigate whatever lay under the great, oak slab. Placing the lantern on the floor, I tumbled the stones off the trap, and, grasping the ring, pulled the door open. As I did so, the cellar became filled with the sound of a murmurous thunder, that rose from far below. At the same time, a damp wind blew up into my face, bringing with it a load of fine spray. Therewith, I dropped the trap, hurriedly, with a half frightened feeling of wonder.

"For a moment, I stood puzzled. I was not particularly afraid. The haunting fear of the Swine-things had left me, long ago; but I was certainly nervous and astonished. Then, a sudden thought possessed me, and I raised the ponderous door, with a feeling of excitement. Leaving it standing upon its end, I seized the lantern, and, kneeling down, thrust it into the opening. As I did so, the moist wind and spray drove in my eyes, making me unable to see, for a few moments. Even when my eyes were clear, I could distinguish nothing below me, save darkness, and whirling spray.

"Seeing that it was useless to expect to make out anything, with the light so high, I felt in my pockets for a piece of twine, with which to lower it further into the opening. Even as I fumbled, the lantern slipped from my fingers, and hurtled down into the darkness. For a brief instant, I watched its fall, and saw the light shine on a tumult of white foam, some eighty or a hundred feet below me. Then it was gone. My sudden surmise was correct, and now, I knew the cause of the wet and noise. The great cellar was connected with the Pit, by means of the trap, which opened right above it; and the moisture, was the spray, rising from the water, falling into the depths.

"In an instant, I had an explanation of certain things, that had hitherto puzzled me. Now, I could understand why the noises—on the first night of the invasion—had seemed to rise directly from under my feet. And the chuckle that had sounded when first I opened the trap! Evidently, some of the Swine-things must have been right beneath me.

"Another thought struck me. Were the creatures all drowned? Would they drown? I remembered how unable I had been to find any traces to show that my shooting had been really fatal. Had they life, as we understand life, or were they ghouls? These thoughts flashed through my brain, as I stood in the dark, searching my pockets for matches. I had the box in my hand now, and, striking a light, I stepped to the trap door, and closed it. Then, I piled the stones back upon it; after which, I made my way out from the cellars.

"And so, I suppose the water goes on, thundering down into that bottomless hell-pit. Sometimes, I have an inexplicable desire to go down to the great cellar, open the trap, and gaze into the impenetrable, spray-damp darkness. At times, the desire becomes almost overpowering, in its intensity. It is not mere curiosity, that prompts me; but more as though some unexplained influence were at work. Still, I never go; and intend to fight down the strange longing, and crush it; even as I would the unholy thought of self-destruction.

"This idea of some intangible force being exerted, may seem reasonless. Yet, my instinct warns me, that it is not so. In these things, reason seems to me less to be trusted than instinct.

"One thought there is, in closing, that impresses itself upon me, with ever growing insistence. It is, that I live in a very strange house; a very awful house. And I have begun to wonder whether I am doing wisely in staying here. Yet, if I left, where could I go, and still obtain the solitude, and the sense of her presence,* that alone make my old life bearable?

* An apparently unmeaning interpolation. I can find no previous reference in the MS. to this matter. It becomes clearer, however, in the light of succeeding incidents.—Ed.

Chapter XIV
The Sea of Sleep

"For a considerable period after the last incident which I have narrated in my diary, I had serious thoughts of leaving this house, and might have done so; but for the great and wonderful thing, of which I am about to write.

"How well I was advised, in my heart, when I stayed on here—spite of those visions and sights of unknown and unexplainable things; for, had I not stayed, then I had not seen again the face of her I loved. Yes, though few know it, none now save my sister Mary, I have loved and, ah! me—lost.

"I would write down the story of those sweet, old days; but it would be like the tearing of old wounds; yet, after that which has happened, what need have I to care? For she has come to me out of the unknown. Strangely, she warned me; warned me passionately against this house; begged me to leave it; but admitted, when I questioned her, that she could not have come to me, had I been elsewhere. Yet, in spite of this, still she warned me, earnestly; telling me that it was a place, long ago given over to evil, and under the power of grim laws, of which none here have knowledge. And I—I just asked her, again, whether she would come to me elsewhere, and she could only stand, silent.

"It was thus, that I came to the place of the Sea of Sleep—so she termed it, in her dear speech with me. I had stayed up, in my study, reading; and must have dozed over the book. Suddenly, I awoke and sat upright, with a start. For a moment, I looked round, with a puzzled sense of something unusual. There was a misty look about the room, giving a curious softness to each table and chair and furnishing.

"Gradually, the mistiness increased; growing, as it were, out of nothing. Then, slowly, a soft, white light began to glow in the room. The flames of the candles shone through it, palely. I looked from side to side, and found that I could still see each piece of furniture; but in a strangely unreal way, more as though the ghost of each table and chair had taken the place of the solid article.

"Gradually, as I looked, I saw them fade and fade; until, slowly, they resolved into nothingness. Now, I looked again at the candles. They shone wanly, and, even as I watched, grew more unreal, and so vanished. The room was filled, now, with a soft, yet luminous, white twilight, like a gentle mist of light. Beyond this, I could see nothing. Even the walls had vanished.

"Presently, I became conscious that a faint, continuous sound, pulsed through the silence that wrapped me. I listened intently. It grew more distinct, until it appeared to me that I harked to the breathings of some great sea. I cannot tell how long a space passed thus; but, after a while, it seemed that I could see through the mistiness; and, slowly, I became aware that I was standing upon the shore of an immense and silent sea. This shore was smooth and long, vanishing to right and left of me, in extreme distances. In front, swam a still immensity of sleeping ocean. At times, it seemed to me that I caught a faint glimmer of light, under its surface; but of this, I could not be sure. Behind me, rose up, to an extraordinary height, gaunt, black cliffs.

"Overhead, the sky was of a uniform cold grey colour—the whole place being lit by a stupendous globe of pale fire, that swam a little above the far horizon, and shed a foam-like light above the quiet waters.

"Beyond the gentle murmur of the sea, an intense stillness prevailed. For a long while, I stayed there, looking out across its strangeness. Then, as I stared, it seemed that a bubble of white foam floated up out of the depths, and then, even now I know not how it was, I was looking upon, nay, looking *into* the face of Her—aye! into her face—into her soul; and she looked back at me, with such a commingling of joy and sadness, that I ran towards her, blindly; crying strangely to her, in a very agony of remembrance, of terror, and of hope, to come to me. Yet, spite of my crying, she stayed out there upon the sea, and only shook her head, sorrowfully; but, in her eyes was the old earth-light of tenderness, that I had come to know, before all things, ere we were parted.

"At her perverseness, I grew desperate, and essayed to wade out to her; yet, though I would, I could not. Something, some invisible barrier, held me back, and I was fain to stay where I was, and cry out to her in the fullness of my soul, 'O, my Darling, my Darling—' but could say no more, for very intensity. And, at that, she came over, swiftly, and touched me, and it was as though heaven had opened. Yet, when I reached out my hands to her, she put me from her with tenderly stern hands, and I was abashed—"

NOTE.— Here, the writing becomes undecipherable, owing to the damaged condition of this part of the MS. Below I print such fragments as are legible.—Ed.

The Fragments

(The legible portions of the mutilated leaves.)

". . . through tears . . . noise of eternity in my ears, we parted . . . She whom I love. O, my God . . . !

"I was a great time dazed, and then I was alone in the blackness of the night. I knew that I journeyed back, once more, to the known universe. Presently, I emerged from that enormous darkness. I had come among the stars . . . vast time . . . the sun, far and remote.

"I entered into the gulf that separates our system from the outer suns. As I sped across the dividing dark, I watched, steadily, the ever-growing brightness and size of our sun. Once, I glanced back to the stars, and saw them shift, as it were, in my wake, against the mighty background of night, so vast was the speed of my passing spirit.

"I drew nigher to our system, and now I could see the shine of Jupiter. Later, I distinguished the cold, blue gleam of the earthlight . . . . I had a moment of bewilderment. All about the sun there seemed to be bright, objects, moving in rapid orbits. Inward, nigh to the savage glory of the sun, there circled two darting points of light, and, further off, there flew a blue, shining speck, that I knew to be the earth. It circled the sun in a space that seemed to be no more than an earth-minute.

" . . . nearer with great speed. I saw the radiances of Jupiter and Saturn, spinning, with incredible swiftness, in huge orbits. And ever I drew more nigh, and looked out upon this strange sight—the visible circling of the planets about the mother sun. It was as though time had been annihilated for me; so that a year was no more to my unfleshed spirit, than is a moment to an earth-bound soul.

"The speed of the planets, appeared to increase; and, presently, I was watching the sun, all ringed about with hair-like circles of different coloured fire—the paths of the planets, hurtling at mighty speed, about the central flame . . . .

" . . . the sun grew vast, as though it leapt to meet me . . . . And now I was within the circling of the outer planets, and flitting swiftly, towards the place where the earth, glimmering through the blue splendour of its orbit, as though a fiery mist, circled the sun at a monstrous speed . . . . "

NOTE.—The severest scrutiny has not enabled me to decipher more of the damaged portion of the MS. It commences to be legible again with the chapter entitled "The Noise in the Night".—Ed.

Chapter XV
The Noise in the Night

"And now, I come to the strangest of all the strange happenings that have befallen me in this house of mysteries. It occurred quite lately—within the month; and I have little doubt but that what I saw was in reality the end of all things. However, to my story.

"I do not know how it is; but, up to the present, I have never been able to write these things down, directly they happened. It is as though I have to wait a time, recovering my just balance, and digesting—as it were—the things I have heard or seen. No doubt, this is as it should be; for, by waiting, I see the incidents more truly, and write of them in a calmer and more judicial frame of mind. This by the way.

"It is now the end of November. My story relates to what happened in the first week of the month.

"It was night, about eleven o'clock. Pepper and I kept one another company in the study—that great, old room of mine, where I read and work. I was reading, curiously enough, the Bible. I have begun, in these later days, to take a growing interest in that great and ancient book. Suddenly, a distinct tremor shook the house, and there came a faint and distant, whirring buzz, that grew rapidly into a far, muffled screaming. It reminded me, in a queer, gigantic way, of the noise that a clock makes, when the catch is released, and it is allowed to run down. The sound appeared to come from some remote height—somewhere up in the night. There was no repetition of the shock. I looked across at Pepper. He was sleeping peacefully.

"Gradually, the whirring noise decreased, and there came a long silence.

"All at once, a glow lit up the end window, which protrudes far out from the side of the house, so that, from it, one may look both East and West. I felt puzzled, and, after a moment's hesitation, walked across the room, and pulled aside the blind. As I did so, I saw the Sun rise, from behind the horizon. It rose with a steady, perceptible movement. I could see it travel upwards. In a minute, it seemed, it had reached the tops of the trees, through which I had watched it. Up, up—It was broad daylight now. Behind me, I was conscious of a sharp, mosquito-like buzzing. I glanced round, and knew that it came from the clock. Even as I looked, it marked off an hour. The minute hand was moving round the dial, faster than an ordinary second-hand. The hour hand moved quickly from space to space. I had a numb sense of astonishment. A moment later, so it seemed, the two candles went out, almost together. I turned swiftly back to the window; for I had seen the shadow of the window-frames, traveling along the floor towards me, as though a great lamp had been carried up past the window.

"I saw now, that the sun had risen high into the heavens, and was still visibly moving. It passed above the house, with an extraordinary sailing kind of motion. As the window came into shadow, I saw another extraordinary thing. The fine-weather clouds were not passing, easily, across the sky—they were scampering, as though a hundred-mile-an-hour wind blew. As they passed, they changed their shapes a thousand times a minute, as though writhing with a strange life; and so were gone. And, presently, others came, and whisked away likewise.

"To the West, I saw the sun, drop with an incredible, smooth, swift motion. Eastward, the shadows of every seen thing crept towards the coming greyness. And the movement of the shadows was visible to me—a stealthy, writhing creep of the shadows of the wind-stirred trees. It was a strange sight.

"Quickly, the room began to darken. The sun slid down to the horizon, and seemed, as it were, to disappear from my sight, almost with a jerk. Through the greyness of the swift evening, I saw the silver crescent of the moon, falling out of the Southern sky, towards the West. The evening seemed to merge into an almost instant night. Above me, the many constellations passed in a strange, 'noiseless' circling, West-ward. The moon fell through that last thousand fathoms of the night-gulf, and there was only the starlight . . . .

"About this time, the buzzing in the corner ceased; telling me that the clock had run down. A few minutes passed, and I saw the Eastward sky lighten. A grey, sullen morning spread through all the darkness, and hid the march of the stars. Overhead, there moved, with a heavy, everlasting rolling, a vast, seamless sky of grey clouds—a cloud-sky that would have seemed motionless, through all the length of an ordinary earth-day. The sun was hidden from me; but, from moment to moment, the world would brighten and darken, brighten and darken, beneath waves of subtle light and shadow . . . .

"The light shifted ever Westward, and the night fell upon the earth. A vast rain seemed to come with it, and a wind of a most extraordinary loudness—as though the howling of a nightlong gale, were packed into the space of no more than a minute.

"This noise passed, almost immediately, and the clouds broke; so that, once more, I could see the sky. The stars were flying Westward, with astounding speed. It came to me now, for the first time, that, though the noise of the wind had passed, yet a constant "blurred" sound was in my ears. Now that I noticed it, I was aware that it had been with me all the time. It was the world-noise.

"And then, even as I grasped at so much comprehension, there came the Eastward light. No more than a few heartbeats, and the sun rose, swiftly. Through the trees, I saw it, and then it was above the trees. Up—up, it soared and all the world was light. It passed, with a swift, steady swing to its highest altitude, and fell thence, Westward. I saw the day roll visibly over my head. A few light clouds flittered Northward, and vanished. The sun went down with one swift, clear plunge, and there was about me, for a few seconds, the darker growing grey of the gloaming.

"Southward and Westward, the moon was sinking rapidly. The night had come, already. A minute it seemed, and the moon fell those remaining fathoms of dark sky. Another minute, or so, and the Eastward sky glowed with the coming dawn. The sun leapt upon me with a frightening abruptness, and soared ever more swiftly towards the zenith. Then, suddenly, a fresh thing came to my sight. A black thundercloud rushed up out of the South, and seemed to leap all the arc of the sky, in a single instant. As it came, I saw that its advancing edge flapped, like a monstrous black cloth in the heaven, twirling and undulating rapidly, with a horrid suggestiveness. In an instant, all the air was full of rain, and a hundred lightning flashes seemed to flood downwards, as it were in one great shower. In the same second of time, the world-noise was drowned in the roar of the wind, and then my ears ached, under the stunning impact of the thunder.

"And, in the midst of this storm, the night came; and then, within the space of another minute, the storm had passed, and there was only the constant 'blur' of the world-noise on my hearing. Overhead, the stars were sliding quickly Westward; and something, mayhaps the particular speed to which they had attained, brought home to me, for the first time, a keen realization of the knowledge that it was the world that revolved. I seemed to see, suddenly, the world—a vast, dark mass—revolving visibly against the stars.

"The dawn and the sun seemed to come together, so greatly had the speed of the world-revolution increased. The sun drove up, in one long, steady curve; passed its highest point, and swept down into the Western sky, and disappeared. I was scarcely conscious of evening, so brief was it. Then I was watching the flying constellations, and the Westward hastening moon. In but a space of seconds, so it seemed, it was sliding swiftly downward through the night-blue, and then was gone. And, almost directly, came the morning.

"And now there seemed to come a strange acceleration. The sun made one clean, clear sweep through the sky, and disappeared behind the Westward horizon, and the night came and went with a like haste.

"As the succeeding day, opened and closed upon the world, I was aware of a sweat of snow, suddenly upon the earth. The night came, and, almost immediately, the day. In the brief leap of the sun, I saw that the snow had vanished; and then, once more, it was night.

"Thus matters were; and, even after the many incredible things that I have seen, I experienced all the time a most profound awe. To see the sun rise and set, within a space of time to be measured by seconds; to watch (after a little) the moon leap—a pale, and ever growing orb—up into the night sky, and glide, with a strange swiftness, through the vast arc of blue; and, presently, to see the sun follow, springing out of the Eastern sky, as though in chase; and then again the night, with the swift and ghostly passing of starry constellations, was all too much to view believingly. Yet, so it was—the day slipping from dawn to dusk, and the night sliding swiftly into day, ever rapidly and more rapidly.

"The last three passages of the sun had shown me a snow-covered earth, which, at night, had seemed, for a few seconds, incredibly weird under the fast-shifting light of the soaring and falling moon. Now, however, for a little space, the sky was hidden, by a sea of swaying, leaden-white clouds, which lightened and blackened, alternately, with the passage of day and night.

"The clouds rippled and vanished, and there was once more before me, the vision of the swiftly leaping sun, and nights that came and went like shadows.

"Faster and faster, spun the world. And now each day and night was completed within the space of but a few seconds; and still the speed increased.

"It was a little later, that I noticed that the sun had begun to have the suspicion of a trail of fire behind it. This was due, evidently, to the speed at which it, apparently, traversed the heavens. And, as the days sped, each one quicker than the last, the sun began to assume the appearance of a vast, flaming comet* flaring across the sky at short, periodic intervals. At night, the moon presented, with much greater truth, a comet-like aspect; a pale, and singularly clear, fast travelling shape of fire, trailing streaks of cold flame. The stars showed now, merely as fine hairs of fire against the dark.

"Once, I turned from the window, and glanced at Pepper. In the flash of a day, I saw that he slept, quietly, and I moved once more to my watching.

"The sun was now bursting up from the Eastern horizon, like a stupendous rocket, seeming to occupy no more than

---

* The Recluse uses this as an illustration, evidently in the sense of the popular conception of a comet.—Ed.

a second or two in hurling from East to West. I could no longer perceive the passage of clouds across the sky, which seemed to have darkened somewhat. The brief nights, appeared to have lost the proper darkness of night; so that the hair-like fire of the flying stars, showed but dimly. As the speed increased, the sun began to sway very slowly in the sky, from South to North, and then, slowly again, from North to South.

"So, amid a strange confusion of mind, the hours passed.

"All this while had Pepper slept. Presently, feeling lonely and distraught, I called to him, softly; but he took no notice. Again, I called, raising my voice slightly; still he moved not. I walked over to where he lay, and touched him with my foot, to rouse him. At the action, gentle though it was, he fell to pieces. That is what happened; he literally and actually crumbled into a mouldering heap of bones and dust.

"For the space of, perhaps a minute, I stared down at the shapeless heap, that had once been Pepper. I stood, feeling stunned. What can have happened? I asked myself; not at once grasping the grim significance of that little hill of ash. Then, as I stirred the heap with my foot, it occurred to me that this could only happen in a great space of time. Years—and years.

"Outside, the weaving, fluttering light held the world. Inside, I stood, trying to understand what it meant—what that little pile of dust and dry bones, on the carpet, meant. But I could not think, coherently.

"I glanced away, round the room, and now, for the first time, noticed how dusty and old the place looked. Dust and dirt everywhere; piled in little heaps in the corners, and spread about upon the furniture. The very carpet, itself, was invisible beneath a coating of the same, all pervading, material. As I walked, little clouds of the stuff rose up from under my footsteps, and assailed my nostrils, with a dry, bitter odour that made me wheeze, huskily.

"Suddenly, as my glance fell again upon Pepper's remains, I stood still, and gave voice to my confusion—questioning, aloud, whether the years were, indeed, passing; whether this, which I had taken to be a form of vision, was, in truth, a reality. I paused. A new thought had struck me. Quickly, but with steps which, for the first time, I noticed, tottered, I went across the room to the great pier-glass, and looked in. It was too covered with grime, to give back any reflection, and, with trembling hands, I began to rub off the dirt. Presently, I could see myself. The thought that had come to me, was confirmed. Instead of the great, hale man, who scarcely looked fifty, I was looking at a bent, decrepit man, whose shoulders stooped, and whose face was wrinkled with the years of a century. The hair—which a few short hours ago had been nearly coal black—was now silvery white. Only the eyes were bright. Gradually, I traced, in that ancient man, a faint resemblance to my self of other days.

"I turned away, and tottered to the window. I knew, now, that I was old, and the knowledge seemed to confirm my trembling walk. For a little space, I stared moodily out into the blurred vista of changeful landscape. Even in that short time, a year passed, and, with a petulant gesture, I left the window. As I did so, I noticed that my hand shook with the palsy of old age; and a short sob choked its way through my lips.

"For a little while, I paced, tremulously, between the window and the table; my gaze wandering hither and thither, uneasily. How dilapidated the room was. Everywhere lay the thick dust—thick, sleepy, and black. The fender was a shape of rust. The chains that held the brass clock-weights, had rusted through long ago, and now the weights lay on the floor beneath; themselves two cones of verdigris.

"As I glanced about, it seemed to me that I could see the very furniture of the room rotting and decaying before my eyes. Nor was this fancy, on my part; for, all at once, the bookshelf, along the sidewall, collapsed, with a cracking and rending of rotten wood, precipitating its contents upon the floor, and filling the room with a smother of dusty atoms.

"How tired I felt. As I walked, it seemed that I could hear my dry joints, creak and crack at every step. I wondered about my sister. Was she dead, as well as Pepper? All had happened so quickly and suddenly. This must be, indeed, the beginning of the end of all things! It occurred to me, to go to look for her; but I felt too weary. And then, she had been so queer about these happenings, of late. Of late! I repeated the words, and laughed, feebly—mirthlessly, as the realisation was borne in upon me that I spoke of a time, half a century gone. Half a century! It might have been twice as long!

"I moved slowly to the window, and looked out once more across the world. I can best describe the passage of day and night, at this period, as a sort of gigantic, ponderous flicker. Moment by moment, the acceleration of time continued; so that, at nights now, I saw the moon, only as a swaying trail of palish fire, that varied from a mere line of light to a nebulous path, and then dwindled again, disappearing periodically.

"The flicker of the days and nights quickened. The days had grown perceptibly darker, and a queer quality of dusk lay, as it were, in the atmosphere. The nights were so much lighter, that the stars were scarcely to be seen, saving here and there an occasional hair-like line of fire, that seemed to sway a little, with the moon.

"Quicker, and ever quicker, ran the flicker of day and night; and, suddenly it seemed, I was aware that the flicker had died out, and, instead, there reigned a comparatively steady light, which was shed upon all the world, from an eternal river of flame that swung up and down, North and South, in stupendous, mighty swings.

"The sky was now grown very much darker, and there was in the blue of it a heavy gloom, as though a vast blackness peered through it upon the earth. Yet, there was in it, also, a strange and awful clearness, and emptiness. Periodically, I had glimpses of a ghostly track of fire that swayed thin and darkly towards the sun-stream; vanished and reappeared. It was the scarcely visible moon-stream.

"Looking out at the landscape, I was conscious again, of a blurring sort of 'flitter', that came either from the light of the ponderous-swinging sun-stream, or was the result of the incredibly rapid changes of the earth's surface. And every few moments, so it seemed, the snow would lie suddenly upon the world, and vanish as abruptly, as though an invisible giant 'flitted' a white sheet off and on the earth.

"Time fled, and the weariness that was mine, grew insupportable. I turned from the window, and walked once across the room, the heavy dust deadening the sound of my footsteps. Each step that I took, seemed a greater effort than the one before. An intolerable ache, knew me in every joint and limb, as I trod my way, with a weary uncertainty.

"By the opposite wall, I came to a weak pause, and wondered, dimly, what was my intent. I looked to my left, and saw my old chair. The thought of sitting in it brought a faint sense of comfort to my bewildered wretchedness. Yet, because I was so weary and old and tired, I would scarcely brace my mind to do anything but stand, and wish myself past those few yards. I rocked, as I stood. The floor, even, seemed a place for rest; but the dust lay so thick and sleepy and black. I turned, with a great effort of will, and made towards my chair. I reached it, with a groan of thankfulness. I sat down.

"Everything about me appeared to be growing dim. It was all so strange and unthought of. Last night, I was a comparatively strong, though elderly man; and now, only a few hours later—! I looked at the little dust-heap that had once been Pepper. Hours! and I laughed, a feeble, bitter laugh; a shrill, cackling laugh, that shocked my dimming senses.

"For a while, I must have dozed. Then I opened my eyes, with a start. Somewhere across the room, there had been a muffled noise of something falling. I looked, and saw, vaguely, a cloud of dust hovering above a pile of *débris*. Nearer the door, something else tumbled, with a crash. It was one of the cupboards; but I was tired, and took little notice. I closed my eyes, and sat there in a state of drowsy, semi-unconsciousness. Once or twice—as though coming through thick mists—I heard noises, faintly. Then I must have slept.

Chapter XVI
The Awakening

"I awoke, with a start. For a moment, I wondered where I was. Then memory came to me . . . .

"The room was still lit with that strange light—half-sun, half-moon, light. I felt refreshed, and the tired, weary ache had left me. I went slowly across to the window, and looked out. Overhead, the river of flame drove up and down, North and South, in a dancing semi-circle of fire. As a mighty sley in the loom of time it seemed—in a sudden fancy of mine—to be beating home the picks of the years. For, so vastly had the passage of time been accelerated, that there was no longer any sense of the sun passing from East to West. The only apparent movement was the North and South beat of the sun-stream, that had become so swift now, as to be better described as a *quiver*.

"As I peered out, there came to me a sudden, inconsequent memory of that last journey among the Outer Worlds.* I remembered the sudden vision that had come to me, as I neared the Solar System, of the fast whirling planets about the sun—as though the governing quality of time had been held in abeyance, and the Machine of a Universe allowed to run down an eternity, in a few moments or hours. The

---

* Evidently referring to something set forth in the missing and mutilated pages. See Fragments, p. 101.—Ed.

memory passed, along with a, but partially comprehended, suggestion that I had been permitted a glimpse into further time spaces. I stared out again, seemingly, at the quake of the sun-stream. The speed seemed to increase, even as I looked. Several lifetimes came and went, as I watched.

"Suddenly, it struck me, with a sort of grotesque seriousness, that I was still alive. I thought of Pepper, and wondered how it was that I had not followed his fate. He had reached the time of his dying, and had passed, probably through sheer length of years. And here was I, alive, hundreds of thousands of centuries after my rightful period of years.

"For, a time, I mused, absently. 'Yesterday—' I stopped, suddenly. Yesterday! There was no yesterday. The yesterday of which I spoke had been swallowed up in the abyss of years, ages gone. I grew dazed with much thinking.

"Presently, I turned from the window, and glanced round the room. It seemed different—strangely, utterly different. Then, I knew what it was that made it appear so strange. It was bare: there was not a piece of furniture in the room; not even a solitary fitting of any sort. Gradually, my amazement went, as I remembered, that this was but the inevitable end of that process of decay, which I had witnessed commencing, before my sleep. Thousands of years! Millions of years!

"Over the floor was spread a deep layer of dust, that reached halfway up to the window-seat. It had grown immeasurably, whilst I slept; and represented the dust of untold ages. Undoubtedly, atoms of the old, decayed furniture helped to swell its bulk; and, somewhere among it all, mouldered the long-ago-dead Pepper.

"All at once, it occurred to me, that I had no recollection of wading knee-deep through all that dust, after I awoke. True, an incredible age of years had passed, since I approached the window; but that was evidently as nothing, compared with the countless spaces of time that, I conceived, had vanished whilst I was sleeping. I remembered now, that I had fallen asleep, sitting in my old chair. Had it gone . . . ? I glanced towards where it had stood. Of course, there was no chair to be seen. I could not satisfy myself, whether it had disappeared, after my waking, or before. If it had mouldered under me, surely, I should have been waked by the collapse. Then I remembered that the thick dust, which covered the floor, would have been sufficient to soften my fall; so that it was quite possible, I had slept upon the dust for a million years or more.

"As these thoughts wandered through my brain, I glanced again, casually, to where the chair had stood. Then, for the first time, I noticed that there were no marks, in the dust, of my footprints, between it and the window. But then, ages of years had passed, since I had awaked—tens of thousands of years!

"My look rested thoughtfully, again upon the place where once had stood my chair. Suddenly, I passed from abstraction to intentness; for there, in its standing place, I made out a long undulation, rounded off with the heavy dust. Yet it was not so much hidden, but that I could tell what had caused it. I knew—and shivered at the knowledge—that it was a human body, ages-dead, lying there, beneath the place where I had slept. It was lying on its right side, its back turned towards me. I could make out and trace each curve and outline, softened, and moulded, as it were, in the black dust. In a vague sort of way, I tried to account for its presence there. Slowly, I began to grow bewildered, as the thought came to me that it lay just about where I must have fallen when the chair collapsed.

"Gradually, an idea began to form itself within my brain; a thought that shook my spirit. It seemed hideous and insupportable; yet it grew upon me, steadily, until it became a conviction. The body under that coating, that shroud of dust, was neither more nor less than my own dead shell. I did not attempt to prove it. I knew it now, and wondered I had not known it all along. I was a bodiless thing.

"Awhile, I stood, trying to adjust my thoughts to this new problem. In time—how many thousands of years, I know not—I attained to some degree of quietude—sufficient to enable me to pay attention to what was transpiring around me.

"Now, I saw that the elongated mound had sunk, collapsed, level with the rest of the spreading dust. And fresh atoms, impalpable, had settled above that mixture of grave-powder, which the aeons had ground. A long while, I stood, turned from the window. Gradually, I grew more collected, while the world slipped across the centuries into the future.

"Presently, I began a survey of the room. Now, I saw that time was beginning its destructive work, even on this strange old building. That it had stood through all the years was, it seemed to me, proof that it was something different from any other house. I do not think, somehow, that I had thought of its decaying. Though, why, I could not have said. It was not until I had meditated upon the matter, for some considerable time, that I fully realised that the extraordinary space of time through which it had stood, was sufficient to have utterly pulverised the very stones of which it was built, had they been taken from any earthly quarry. Yes, it was undoubtedly mouldering now. All the plaster had gone from the walls; even as the woodwork of the room had gone, many ages before.

"While I stood, in contemplation, a piece of glass, from one of the small, diamond-shaped panes, dropped, with a dull tap, amid the dust upon the sill behind me, and crumbled into a little heap of powder. As I turned from contemplating it, I saw light between a couple of the stones that formed the outer wall. Evidently, the mortar was falling away . . . .

"After a while, I turned once more to the window, and peered out. I discovered, now, that the speed of time had become enormous. The lateral quiver of the sun-stream, had grown so swift as to cause the dancing semi-circle of flame to merge into, and disappear in, a sheet of fire that covered half the Southern sky from East to West.

"From the sky, I glanced down to the gardens. They were just a blur of a palish, dirty green. I had a feeling that they stood higher, than in the old days; a feeling that they were nearer my window, as though they had risen, bodily. Yet, they were still a long way below me; for the rock, over the mouth of the pit, on which this house stands, arches up to a great height.

"It was later, that I noticed a change in the constant colour of the gardens. The pale, dirty green was growing ever paler and paler, towards white. At last, after a great space, they became greyish-white, and stayed thus for a very long time. Finally, however, the greyness began to fade, even as had the green, into a dead white. And this remained, constant and unchanged. And by this I knew that, at last, snow lay upon all the Northern world.

"And so, by millions of years, time winged onward through eternity, to the end—the end, of which, in the old-earth days, I had thought remotely, and in hazily speculative fashion. And now, it was approaching in a manner of which none had ever dreamed.

"I recollect that, about this time, I began to have a lively, though morbid, curiosity, as to what would happen when the end came—but I seemed strangely without imaginings.

"All this while, the steady process of decay was continuing. The few remaining pieces of glass, had long ago vanished; and, every now and then, a soft thud, and a little cloud of rising dust, would tell of some fragment of fallen mortar or stone.

"I looked up again, to the fiery sheet that quaked in the heavens above me and far down into the Southern sky. As I looked, the impression was borne in upon me, that it had lost some of its first brilliancy—that it was duller, deeper hued.

"I glanced down, once more, to the blurred white of the worldscape. Sometimes, my look returned to the burning sheet of dulling flame, that was, and yet hid, the sun. At times, I glanced behind me, into the growing dusk of the great, silent room, with its aeon-carpet of sleeping dust . . . .

"So, I watched through the fleeting ages, lost in soul-wearing thoughts and wonderings, and possessed with a new weariness.

Chapter XVII
The Slowing Rotation

"It might have been a million years later, that I perceived, beyond possibility of doubt, that the fiery sheet that lit the world, was indeed darkening.

"Another vast space went by, and the whole enormous flame had sunk to a deep, copper colour. Gradually, it darkened, from copper to copper-red, and from this, at times, to a deep, heavy, purplish tint, with, in it, a strange loom of blood.

"Although the light was decreasing, I could perceive no diminishment in the apparent speed of the sun. It still spread itself in that dazzling veil of speed.

"The world, so much of it as I could see, had assumed a dreadful shade of gloom, as though, in very deed, the last day of the worlds approached.

"The sun was dying; of that there could be little doubt; and still the earth whirled onward, through space and all the aeons. At this time, I remember, an extraordinary sense of bewilderment took me. I found myself, later, wandering, mentally, amid an odd chaos of fragmentary modern theories and the old Biblical story of the world's ending.

"Then, for the first time, there flashed across me, the memory that the sun, with its system of planets, was, and had been, traveling through space at an incredible speed. Abruptly, the question rose—*Where?* For a very great time, I pondered this matter; but, finally, with a certain sense of the futility of my puzzlings, I let my thoughts wander to other things. I grew to wondering, how much longer the house would stand. Also, I queried, to myself, whether I should be doomed to stay, bodiless, upon the earth, through the dark-time that I knew was coming. From these thoughts, I fell again to speculations upon the possible direction of the sun's journey through space. . . . And so another great while passed.

"Gradually, as time fled, I began to feel the chill of a great winter. Then, I remembered that, with the sun dying, the cold must be, necessarily, extraordinarily intense. Slowly, slowly, as the aeons slipped into eternity, the earth sank into a heavier and redder gloom. The dull flame in the firmament took on a deeper tint, very sombre and turbid.

"Then, at last, it was borne upon me that there was a change. The fiery, gloomy curtain of flame that hung quaking overhead, and down away into the Southern sky, began to thin and contract; and, in it, as one sees the fast vibrations of a jarred harp-string, I saw once more the sun-stream quivering, giddily, North and South.

"Slowly, the likeness to a sheet of fire, disappeared, and I saw, plainly, the slowing beat of the sun-stream. Yet, even then, the speed of its swing was inconceivably swift. And all the time, the brightness of the fiery arc grew ever duller. Underneath, the world loomed dimly—an indistinct, ghostly region.

"Overhead, the river of flame swayed slower, and even slower; until, at last, it swung to the North and South in great, ponderous beats, that lasted through seconds. A long space went by, and now each sway of the great belt lasted nigh a minute; so that, after a great while, I ceased to distinguish it as a visible movement; and the streaming fire ran in a steady river of dull flame, across the deadly-looking sky.

"An indefinite period passed, and it seemed that the arc of fire became less sharply defined. It appeared to me to grow more attenuated, and I thought blackish streaks showed, occasionally. Presently, as I watched, the smooth onward-flow ceased; and I was able to perceive that there came a momentary, but regular, darkening of the world. This grew until, once more, night descended, in short, but periodic, intervals upon the wearying earth.

"Longer and longer became the nights, and the days equalled them; so that, at last, the day and the night grew to the duration of seconds in length, and the sun showed, once more, like an almost invisible, coppery-red coloured ball, within the glowing mistiness of its flight. Corresponding to the dark lines, showing at times in its trail, there were now distinctly to be seen on the half-visible sun itself, great, dark belts.

"Year after year flashed into the past, and the days and nights spread into minutes. The sun had ceased to have the appearance of a tail; and now rose and set—a tremendous globe of a glowing copper-bronze hue; in parts ringed with blood-red bands; in others, with the dusky ones, that I have already mentioned. These circles—both red and black— were of varying thicknesses. For a time, I was at a loss to account for their presence. Then it occurred to me, that it was scarcely likely that the sun would cool evenly all over; and that these markings were due, probably, to differences in temperature of the various areas; the red representing those parts where the heat was still fervent, and the black those portions which were already comparatively cool.

"It struck me, as a peculiar thing, that the sun should cool in evenly defined rings; until I remembered that, possibly, they were but isolated patches, to which the enormous rotatory speed of the sun had imparted a belt-like appearance. The sun, itself, was very much greater than the sun I had known in the old-world days; and, from this, I argued that it was considerably nearer.

"At nights, the moon* still showed; but small and remote; and the light she reflected was so dull and weak that she seemed little more than the small, dim ghost of the olden moon, that I had known.

"Gradually, the days and nights lengthened out, until they equalled a space somewhat less than one of the old-earth hours; the sun rising and setting like a great, ruddy bronze disk, crossed with ink-black bars. About this time, I found myself, able once more, to see the gardens, with clearness. For the world had now grown very still, and changeless. Yet, I am not correct in saying, 'gardens'; for there were no gardens—nothing that I knew or recognised. In place thereof, I looked out upon a vast plain, stretching away into distance. A little to my left, there was a low range of hills. Everywhere, there was a uniform, white covering of snow, in places rising into hummocks and ridges.

"It was only now, that I recognised how really great had been the snowfall. In places it was vastly deep, as was witnessed by a great, up-leaping, wave-shaped hill, away to my right; though it is not impossible, that this was due, in part, to some rise in the surface of the ground. Strangely enough, the range of low hills to my left—already mentioned—was not entirely covered with the universal snow; instead, I could see their bare, dark sides showing in several places. And everywhere and always there reigned an incredible death-silence and desolation. The immutable, awful quiet of a dying world.

"All this time, the days and nights were lengthening, perceptibly. Already, each day occupied, maybe, some two

---

* No further mention is made of the moon. From what is said here, it is evident that our satellite had greatly increased its distance from the earth. Possibly, at a later age it may even have broken loose from our attraction. I cannot but regret that no light is shed on this point.—Ed.

hours from dawn to dusk. At night, I had been surprised to find that there were very few stars overhead, and these small, though of an extraordinary brightness; which I attributed to the peculiar, but clear, blackness of the night-time.

"Away to the North, I could discern a nebulous sort of mistiness; not unlike, in appearance, a small portion of the Milky Way. It might have been an extremely remote star-cluster; or—the thought came to me suddenly—perhaps it was the sidereal universe that I had known, and now left far behind, forever—a small, dimly glowing mist of stars, far in the depths of space.

"Still, the days and nights lengthened, slowly. Each time, the sun rose duller than it had set. And the dark belts increased in breadth.

"About this time, there happened a fresh thing. The sun, earth, and sky were suddenly darkened, and, apparently, blotted out for a brief space. I had a sense, a certain awareness (I could learn little by sight), that the earth was enduring a very great fall of snow. Then, in an instant, the veil that had obscured everything, vanished, and I looked out, once more. A marvellous sight met my gaze. The hollow in which this house, with its gardens, stands, was brimmed with snow.* It lipped over the sill of my window. Everywhere, it lay, a great level stretch of white, which caught and reflected, gloomily, the sombre coppery glows of the dying sun. The world had become a shadowless plain, from horizon to horizon.

"I glanced up at the sun. It shone with an extraordinary, dull clearness. I saw it, now, as one who, until then, had seen it, only through a partially obscuring medium. All about it, the sky had become black, with a clear, deep blackness, frightful in its nearness, and its unmeasured deep, and

* Conceivably, frozen air.—Ed.

its utter unfriendliness. For a great time, I looked into it, newly, and shaken and fearful. It was so near. Had I been a child, I might have expressed some of my sensation and distress, by saying that the sky had lost its roof.

"Later, I turned, and peered about me, into the room. Everywhere, it was covered with a thin shroud of the all-pervading white. I could see it but dimly, by reason of the sombre light that now lit the world. It appeared to cling to the ruined walls; and the thick, soft dust of the years, that covered the floor knee-deep, was nowhere visible. The snow must have blown in through the open framework of the windows. Yet, in no place had it drifted; but lay everywhere about the great, old room, smooth and level. Moreover, there had been no wind these many thousand years. But there was the snow,* as I have told.

"And all the earth was silent. And there was a cold, such as no living man can ever have known.

"The earth was now illuminated, by day, with a most doleful light, beyond my power to describe. It seemed as though I looked at the great plain, through the medium of a bronze-tinted sea.

"It was evident that the earth's rotatory movement was departing, steadily.

"The end came, all at once. The night had been the longest yet; and when the dying sun showed, at last, above the world's edge, I had grown so wearied of the dark, that I greeted it as a friend. It rose steadily, until about twenty degrees above the horizon. Then, it stopped suddenly, and, after a strange retrograde movement, hung motionless—a great shield in the sky.** Only the circular rim of the sun

* See previous footnote. This would explain the snow (?) within the room.—Ed.

** I am confounded that neither here, nor later on, does the showed bright—only this, and one thin streak of light near the equator.

"Gradually, even this thread of light died out; and now, all that was left of our great and glorious sun, was a vast dead disk, rimmed with a thin circle of bronze-red light.

Recluse make any further mention of the continued north and south movement (apparent, of course,) of the sun from solstice to solstice.—Ed.

Chapter XVIII
The Green Star

"The world was held in a savage gloom—cold and intolerable. Outside, all was quiet—quiet! From the dark room behind me, came the occasional, soft thud* of falling matter—fragments of rotting stone. So time passed, and night grasped the world, wrapping it in wrappings of impenetrable blackness.

"There was no night-sky, as we know it. Even the few straggling stars had vanished, conclusively. I might have been in a shuttered room, without a light; for all that I could see. Only, in the impalpableness of gloom, opposite, burnt that vast, encircling hair of dull fire. Beyond this, there was no ray in all the vastitude of night that surrounded me; save that, far in the North, that soft, mist-like glow still shone.

"Silently, years moved on. What period of time passed, I shall never know. It seemed to me, waiting there, that eternities came and went, stealthily; and still I watched. I could see only the glow of the sun's edge, at times; for now,

---

* At this time the sound-carrying atmosphere must have been either incredibly attenuated, or—more probably—non-existent. In the light of this, it cannot be supposed that these, or any other, noises would have been apparent to living ears—to hearing, as we, in the material body, understand that sense.—Ed.

it had commenced to come and go—lighting up a while, and again becoming extinguished.

"All at once, during one of these periods of life, a sudden flame cut across the night—a quick glare that lit up the dead earth, shortly; giving me a glimpse of its flat lonesomeness. The light appeared to come from the sun—shooting out from somewhere near its centre, diagonally. A moment, I gazed, startled. Then the leaping flame sank, and the gloom fell again. But now it was not so dark; and the sun was belted by a thin line of vivid, white light. I stared, intently. Had a volcano broken out on the sun? Yet, I negatived the thought, as soon as formed. I felt that the light had been far too intensely white, and large, for such a cause.

"Another idea there was, that suggested itself to me. It was, that one of the inner planets had fallen into the sun—becoming incandescent, under that impact. This theory appealed to me, as being more plausible, and accounting more satisfactorily for the extraordinary size and brilliance of the blaze, that had lit up the dead world, so unexpectedly.

"Full of interest and emotion, I stared, across the darkness, at that line of white fire, cutting the night. One thing it told to me, unmistakably: the sun was yet rotating at an enormous speed.* Thus, I knew that the years were still fleeting at an incalculable rate; though so far as the earth was concerned, life, and light, and time, were things belonging to a period lost in the long gone ages.

"After that one burst of flame, the light had shown, only as an encircling band of bright fire. Now, however, as I watched, it began slowly to sink into a ruddy tint, and, later, to a dark, copper-red colour; much as the sun had done.

---

* I can only suppose that the time of the earth's yearly journey had ceased to bear its present relative proportion to the period of the sun's rotation.—Ed.

Presently, it sank to a deeper hue; and, in a still further space of time, it began to fluctuate; having periods of glowing, and anon, dying. Thus, after a great while, it disappeared.

"Long before this, the smouldering edge of the sun had deadened into blackness. And so, in that supremely future time, the world, dark and intensely silent, rode on its gloomy orbit around the ponderous mass of the dead sun.

"My thoughts, at this period, can be scarcely described. At first, they were chaotic and wanting in coherence. But, later, as the ages came and went, my soul seemed to imbibe the very essence of the oppressive solitude and dreariness, that held the earth.

"With this feeling, there came a wonderful clearness of thought, and I realised, despairingly, that the world might wander for ever, through that enormous night. For a while, the unwholesome idea filled me, with a sensation of over-bearing desolation; so that I could have cried like a child. In time, however, this feeling grew, almost insensibly, less, and an unreasoning hope possessed me. Patiently, I waited.

"From time to time, the noise of dropping particles, behind in the room, came dully to my ears. Once, I heard a loud crash, and turned, instinctively, to look; forgetting, for the moment, the impenetrable night in which every detail was submerged. In a while, my gaze sought the heavens; turning, unconsciously, towards the North. Yes, the nebulous glow still showed. Indeed, I could have almost imagined that it looked somewhat plainer. For a long time, I kept my gaze fixed upon it; feeling, in my lonely soul, that its soft haze was, in some way, a tie with the past. Strange, the trifles from which one can suck comfort! And yet, had I but known—But I shall come to that in its proper time.

"For a very long space, I watched, without experiencing any of the desire for sleep, that would so soon have visited me in the old-earth days. How I should have welcomed it; if only to have passed the time, away from my perplexities and thoughts.

"Several times, the comfortless sound of some great piece of masonry falling, disturbed my meditations; and, once, it seemed I could hear whispering in the room, behind me. Yet it was utterly useless to try to see anything. Such blackness, as existed, scarcely can be conceived. It was palpable, and hideously brutal to the sense; as though something dead, pressed up against me—something soft, and icily cold.

"Under all this, there grew up within my mind, a great and overwhelming distress of uneasiness, that left me, but to drop me into an uncomfortable brooding. I felt that I must fight against it; and, presently, hoping to distract my thoughts, I turned to the window, and looked up towards the North, in search of the nebulous whiteness, which, still, I believed to be the far and misty glowing of the universe we had left. Even as I raised my eyes, I was thrilled with a feeling of wonder; for, now, the hazy light had resolved into a single, great star, of vivid green.

"As I stared, astonished, the thought flashed into my mind; that the earth must be travelling towards the star; not away, as I had imagined. Next, that it could not be the universe the earth had left; but, possibly, an outlying star, belonging to some vast star-cluster, hidden in the enormous depths of space. With a sense of commingled awe and curiosity, I watched it, wondering what new thing was to be revealed to me.

"For a while, vague thoughts and speculations occupied me, during which my gaze dwelt insatiably upon that one spot of light, in the otherwise pit-like darkness. Hope grew up within me, banishing the oppression of despair, that had seemed to stifle me. Wherever the earth was travelling, it was, at least, going once more towards the realms of light. Light! One must spend an eternity wrapped in soundless night, to understand the full horror of being without it.

135

"Slowly, but surely, the star grew upon my vision, until, in time, it shone as brightly as had the planet Jupiter, in the old-earth days. With increased size, its colour became more impressive; reminding me of a huge emerald, scintillating rays of fire across the world.

"Years fled away in silence, and the green star grew into a great splash of flame in the sky. A little later, I saw a thing that filled me with amazement. It was the ghostly outline of a vast crescent, in the night; a gigantic new moon, seeming to be growing out of the surrounding gloom. Utterly bemused, I stared at it. It appeared to be quite close—comparatively; and I puzzled to understand how the earth had come so near to it, without my having seen it before.

"The light, thrown by the star, grew stronger; and, presently, I was aware that it was possible to see the earthscape again; though indistinctly. Awhile, I stared, trying to make out whether I could distinguish any detail of the world's surface, but I found the light insufficient. In a little, I gave up the attempt, and glanced once more towards the star. Even in the short space, that my attention had been diverted, it had increased considerably, and seemed now, to my bewildered sight, about a quarter of the size of the full moon. The light it threw, was extraordinarily powerful; yet its colour was so abominably unfamiliar, that such of the world as I could see, showed unreal; more as though I looked out upon a landscape of shadow, than aught else.

"All this time, the great crescent was increasing in brightness, and began, now, to shine with a perceptible shade of green. Steadily, the star increased in size and brilliancy, until it showed, fully as large as half a full moon; and, as it grew greater and brighter, so did the vast crescent throw out more and more light, though of an ever deepening hue of green. Under the combined blaze of their radiances, the wilderness that stretched before me, became steadily more visible. Soon, I seemed able to stare across the whole world, which now appeared, beneath the strange light, terrible in its cold and awful, flat dreariness.

"It was a little later, that my attention was drawn to the fact, that the great star of green flame, was slowly sinking out of the North, towards the East. At first, I could scarcely believe that I saw aright; but soon there could be no doubt that it was so. Gradually, it sank, and, as it fell, the vast crescent of glowing green, began to dwindle and dwindle, until it became a mere arc of light, against the livid coloured sky. Later it vanished, disappearing in the self-same spot from which I had seen it slowly emerge.

"By this time, the star had come to within some thirty degrees of the hidden horizon. In size it could now have rivalled the moon at its full; though, even yet, I could not distinguish its disk. This fact led me to conceive that it was, still, an extraordinary distance away; and, this being so, I knew that its size must be huge, beyond the conception of man to understand or imagine.

"Suddenly, as I watched, the lower edge of the star vanished—cut by a straight, dark line. A minute—or a century—passed, and it dipped lower, until the half of it had disappeared from sight. Far away out on the great plain, I saw a monstrous shadow blotting it out, and advancing swiftly. Only a third of the star was visible now. Then, like a flash, the solution of this extraordinary phenomenon revealed itself to me. The star was sinking behind the enormous mass of the dead sun. Or rather, the sun—obedient to its attraction—was rising towards it,* with the earth following in its trail. As these

* A careful reading of the MS. suggests that, either the sun is travelling on an orbit of great eccentricity, or else that it was approaching the green star on a lessening orbit. And at this moment, I conceive it to be finally torn directly from its oblique course, by the gravitational pull of the immense star.—Ed.

thoughts expanded in my mind, the star vanished; being completely hidden by the tremendous bulk of the sun. Over the earth there fell, once more, the brooding night.

"With the darkness, came an intolerable feeling of loneliness and dread. For the first time, I thought of the Pit, and its inmates. After that, there rose in my memory the still more terrible Thing, that had haunted the shores of the Sea of Sleep, and lurked in the shadows of this old building. Where were they? I wondered—and shivered with miserable thoughts. For a time, fear held me, and I prayed, wildly and incoherently, for some ray of light with which to dispel the cold blackness that enveloped the world.

"How long I waited, it is impossible to say—certainly for a very great period. Then, all at once, I saw a loom of light shine out ahead. Gradually, it became more distinct. Suddenly, a ray of vivid green, flashed across the darkness. At the same moment, I saw a thin line of livid flame, far in the night. An instant, it seemed, and it had grown into a great clot of fire; beneath which, the world lay bathed in a blaze of emerald green light. Steadily it grew, until, presently, the whole of the green star had come into sight again. But now, it could be scarcely called a star; for it had increased to vast proportions, being incomparably greater than the sun had been in the olden time.

"Then, as I stared, I became aware that I could see the edge of the lifeless sun, glowing like a great crescent-moon. Slowly, its lighted surface, broadened out to me, until half of its diameter was visible; and the star began to drop away on my right. Time passed, and the earth moved on, slowly traversing the tremendous face of the dead sun.*

---

* It will be noticed here that the earth was "slowly traversing the tremendous face of the dead sun". No explanation is given of this, and we must conclude, either that the speed of time had slowed,

"Gradually, as the earth travelled forward, the star fell still more to the right; until, at last, it shone on the back of the house, sending a flood of broken rays, in through the skeleton-like walls. Glancing upwards, I saw that much of the ceiling had vanished, enabling me to see that the upper storeys were even more decayed. The roof had, evidently, gone entirely; and I could see the green effulgence of the Starlight shining in, slantingly.

or else that the earth was actually progressing on its orbit at a rate, slow, when measured by existing standards. A careful study of the MS. however, leads me to conclude that the speed of time had been steadily decreasing for a very considerable period.—Ed.

Chapter XIX
The End of the Solar System

"From the abutment, where once had been the windows, through which I had watched that first, fatal dawn, I could see that the sun was hugely greater, than it had been, when first the Star lit the world. So great was it, that its lower edge seemed almost to touch the far horizon. Even as I watched, I imagined that it drew closer. The radiance of green that lit the frozen earth, grew steadily brighter.

"Thus, for a long space, things were. Then, on a sudden, I saw that the sun was changing shape, and growing smaller, just as the moon would have done in past time. In a while, only a third of the illuminated part was turned towards the earth. The Star bore away on the left.

"Gradually, as the world moved on, the Star shone upon the front of the house, once more; while the sun showed, only as a great bow of green fire. An instant, it seemed, and the sun had vanished. The Star was still fully visible. Then the earth moved into the black shadow of the sun, and all was night—Night, black, starless, and intolerable.

"Filled with tumultuous thoughts, I watched across the night—waiting. Years, it may have been, and then, in the dark house behind me, the clotted stillness of the world was broken. I seemed to hear a soft padding of many feet, and a faint, inarticulate whisper of sound, grew on my sense.

I looked round into the blackness, and saw a multitude of eyes. As I stared, they increased, and appeared to come towards me. For an instant, I stood, unable to move. Then a hideous swine-noise* rose up into the night; and, at that, I leapt from the window, out on to the frozen world. I have a confused notion of having run awhile; and, after that, I just waited—waited. Several times, I heard shrieks; but always as though from a distance. Except for these sounds, I had no idea of the whereabouts of the house. Time moved onward. I was conscious of little, save a sensation of cold and hopelessness and fear.

"An age, it seemed, and there came a glow, that told of the coming light. It grew, tardily. Then—with a loom of unearthly glory—the first ray from the Green Star, struck over the edge of the dark sun, and lit the world. It fell upon a great, ruined structure, some two hundred yards away. It was the house. Staring, I saw a fearsome sight—over its walls crawled a legion of unholy things, almost covering the old building, from tottering towers to base. I could see them, plainly; they were the Swine-creatures.

"The world moved out into the light of the Star, and I saw that, now, it seemed to stretch across a quarter of the heavens. The glory of its livid light was so tremendous, that it appeared to fill the sky with quivering flames. Then, I saw the sun. It was so close that half of its diameter lay below the horizon; and, as the world circled across its face, it seemed to tower right up into the sky, a stupendous dome of emerald coloured fire. From time to time, I glanced towards the house; but the Swine-things seemed unaware of my proximity.

"Years appeared to pass, slowly. The earth had almost reached the centre of the sun's disk. The light from the

* See footnote, page 128.

Green *Sun*—as now it must be called—shone through the interstices, that gapped the mouldered walls of the old house, giving them the appearance of being wrapped in green flames. The Swine-creatures still crawled about the walls.

"Suddenly, there rose a loud roar of swine-voices, and, up from the centre of the roofless house, shot a vast column of blood-red flame. I saw the little, twisted towers and turrets flash into fire; yet still preserving their twisted crookedness. The beams of the Green Sun, beat upon the house, and intermingled with its lurid glows; so that it appeared a blazing furnace of red and green fire.

"Fascinated, I watched, until an overwhelming sense of coming danger, drew my attention. I glanced up, and, at once, it was borne upon me, that the sun was closer; so close, in fact, that it seemed to overhang the world. Then—I know not how—I was caught up into strange heights—floating like a bubble in the awful effulgence.

"Far below me, I saw the earth, with the burning house leaping into an ever growing mountain of flame, round about it, the ground appeared to be glowing; and, in places, heavy wreaths of yellow smoke ascended from the earth. It seemed as though the world were becoming ignited from that one plague-spot of fire. Faintly, I could see the Swine-things. They appeared quite unharmed. Then the ground seemed to cave in, suddenly, and the house, with its load of foul creatures, disappeared into the depths of the earth, sending a strange, blood coloured cloud into the heights. I remembered the hell Pit under the house.

"In a while, I looked round. The huge bulk of the sun, rose high above me. The distance between it and the earth, grew rapidly less. Suddenly, the earth appeared to shoot forward. In a moment, it had traversed the space between it and the sun. I heard no sound; but, out from the sun's face, gushed an ever-growing tongue of dazzling flame. It seemed to leap, almost to the distant Green Sun—shearing through the emerald light, a very cataract of blinding fire. It reached its limit, and sank; and, on the sun, glowed a vast splash of burning white—the grave of the earth.

"The sun was very close to me, now. Presently, I found that I was rising higher; until, at last, I rode above it, in the emptiness. The Green Sun was now so huge that its breadth seemed to fill up all the sky, ahead. I looked down, and noted that the sun was passing directly beneath me.

"A year may have gone by—or a century—and I was left, suspended, alone. The sun showed far in front—a black, circular mass, against the molten splendour of the great, Green Orb. Near one edge, I observed that a lurid glow had appeared, marking the place where the earth had fallen. By this, I knew that the long-dead sun was still revolving, though with great slowness.

"Afar to my right, I seemed to catch, at times, a faint glow of whitish light. For a great time, I was uncertain whether to put this down to fancy or not. Thus, for a while, I stared, with fresh wonderings; until, at last, I knew that it was no imaginary thing; but a reality. It grew brighter; and, presently, there slid out of the green, a pale globe of softest white. It came nearer, and I saw that it was apparently surrounded by a robe of gently glowing clouds. Time passed . . . .

"I glanced towards the diminishing sun. It showed, only as a dark blot on the face of the Green Sun. As I watched, I saw it grow smaller, steadily, as though rushing towards the superior orb, at an immense speed. Intently, I stared. What would happen? I was conscious of extraordinary emotions, as I realised that it would strike the Green Sun. It grew no bigger than a pea, and I looked, with my whole soul, to witness the final end of our System—that system which had borne the world through so many aeons, with its multitudinous sorrows and joys; and now—

"Suddenly, something crossed my vision, cutting from sight all vestige of the spectacle I watched with such soul-interest. What happened to the dead sun, I did not see; but I have no reason—in the light of that which I saw afterwards—to disbelieve that it fell into the strange fire of the Green Sun, and so perished.

"And then, suddenly, an extraordinary question rose in my mind, whether this stupendous globe of green fire might not be the vast Central Sun—the great sun, round which our universe and countless others revolve. I felt confused. I thought of the probable end of the dead sun, and another suggestion came, dumbly—Do the dead stars make the Green Sun their grave? The idea appealed to me with no sense of grotesqueness; but rather as something both possible and probable.

Chapter XX
The Celestial Globes

"For a while, many thoughts crowded my mind, so that I was unable to do aught, save stare, blindly, before me. I seemed whelmed in a sea of doubt and wonder and sorrowful remembrance.

"It was later, that I came out of my bewilderment. I looked about, dazedly. Thus, I saw so extraordinary a sight that, for a while, I could scarcely believe I was not still wrapped in the visionary tumult of my own thoughts. Out of the reigning green, had grown a boundless river of softly shimmering globes—each one enfolded in a wondrous fleece of pure cloud. They reached, both above and below me, to an unknown distance; and, not only hid the shining of the Green Sun; but supplied, in place thereof, a tender glow of light, that suffused itself around me, like unto nothing I have ever seen, before or since.

"In a little, I noticed that there was about these spheres, a sort of transparency, almost as though they were formed of clouded crystal, within which burned a radiance—gentle and subdued. They moved on, past me, continually, floating onward at no great speed; but rather as though they had eternity before them. A great while, I watched, and could perceive no end to them. At times, I seemed to distinguish faces, amid the cloudiness; but strangely indistinct, as though partly real, and partly formed of the mistiness through which they showed.

"For a long time, I waited, passively, with a sense of growing content. I had no longer that feeling of unutterable loneliness; but felt, rather, that I was less alone, than I had been for kalpas of years. This feeling of contentment, increased, so that I would have been satisfied to float in company with those celestial globules, forever.

"Ages slipped by, and I saw the shadowy faces, with increased frequency, also with greater plainness. Whether this was due to my soul having become more attuned to its surroundings, I cannot tell—probably it was so. But, however this may be, I am assured now, only of the fact that I became steadily more conscious of a new mystery about me, telling me that I had, indeed, penetrated within the borderland of some unthought-of region—some subtle, intangible place, or form, of existence.

"The enormous stream of luminous spheres continued to pass me, at an unvarying rate—countless millions; and still they came, showing no signs of ending, nor even diminishing.

"Then, as I was borne, silently, upon the unbuoying ether, I felt a sudden, irresistible, forward movement, towards one of the passing globes. An instant, and I was beside it. Then, I slid through, into the interior, without experiencing the least resistance, of any description. For a short while, I could see nothing; and waited, curiously.

"All at once, I became aware that a sound broke the inconceivable stillness. It was like the murmur of a great sea at calm—a sea breathing in its sleep. Gradually, the mist that obscured my sight, began to thin away; and so, in time, my vision dwelt once again upon the silent surface of the Sea of Sleep.

"For a little, I gazed, and could scarcely believe I saw aright. I glanced round. There was the great globe of pale fire, swimming, as I had seen it before, a short distance above the dim horizon. To my left, far across the sea, I discovered, presently, a faint line, as of thin haze, which I guessed to be the shore, where my Love and I had met, during those wonderful periods of soul-wandering, that had been granted to me in the old earth days.

"Another, a troubled, memory came to me—of the Formless Thing that had haunted the shores of the Sea of Sleep. The guardian of that silent, echoless place. These, and other, details, I remembered, and knew, without doubt that I was looking out upon that same sea. With the assurance, I was filled with an overwhelming feeling of surprise, and joy, and shaken expectancy, conceiving it possible that I was about to see my Love, again. Intently, I gazed around; but could catch no sight of her. At that, for a little, I felt hopeless. Fervently, I prayed, and ever peered, anxiously . . . . How still was the sea!

"Down, far beneath me, I could see the many trails of changeful fire, that had drawn my attention, formerly. Vaguely, I wondered what caused them; also, I remembered that I had intended to ask my dear One about them, as well as many other matters—and I had been forced to leave her, before the half that I had wished to say, was said.

"My thoughts came back with a leap. I was conscious that something had touched me. I turned quickly. God, Thou wert indeed gracious—it was She! She looked up into my eyes, with an eager longing, and I looked down to her, with all my soul. I should like to have held her; but the glorious purity of her face, kept me afar. Then, out of the winding mist, she put her dear arms. Her whisper came to me, soft as the rustle of a passing cloud. 'Dearest!' she said. That was all; but I had heard, and, in a moment I held her to me—as I prayed—forever.

"In a little, she spoke of many things, and I listened. Willingly, would I have done so through all the ages that are to come. At times, I whispered back, and my whispers brought to her spirit face, once more, an indescribably delicate tint—the bloom of love. Later, I spoke more freely, and to each word she listened, and made answer, delightfully; so that, already, I was in Paradise.

"She and I; and nothing, save the silent, spacious void to see us; and only the quiet waters of the Sea of Sleep to hear us.

"Long before, the floating multitude of cloud-enfolded spheres had vanished into nothingness. Thus, we looked upon the face of the slumberous deeps, and were alone. Alone, God, I would be thus alone in the hereafter, and yet be never lonely! I had her, and, greater than this, she had me. Aye, aeon-aged me; and on this thought, and some others, I hope to exist through the few remaining years that may yet lie between us.

Chapter XXI
The Dark Sun

"How long our souls lay in the arms of joy, I cannot say; but, all at once, I was waked from my happiness, by a diminution of the pale and gentle light that lit the Sea of Sleep. I turned towards the huge, white orb, with a premonition of coming trouble. One side of it was curving inward, as though a convex, black shadow were sweeping across it. My memory went back. It was thus, that the darkness had come, before our last parting. I turned towards my Love, inquiringly. With a sudden knowledge of woe, I noticed how wan and unreal she had grown, even in that brief space. Her voice seemed to come to me from a distance. The touch of her hands was no more than the gentle pressure of a summer wind, and grew less perceptible.

"Already, quite half of the immense globe was shrouded. A feeling of desperation seized me. Was she about to leave me? Would she have to go, as she had gone before? I questioned her, anxiously, frightenedly; and she, nestling closer, explained, in that strange, faraway voice, that it was imperative she should leave me, before the Sun of Darkness—as she termed it—blotted out the light. At this confirmation of my fears, I was overcome with despair; and could only look, voicelessly, across the quiet plains of the silent sea.

"How swiftly the darkness spread across the face of the White Orb. Yet, in reality, the time must have been long, beyond human comprehension.

"At last, only a crescent of pale fire, lit the, now dim, Sea of Sleep. All this while, she had held me; but, with so soft a caress, that I had been scarcely conscious of it. We waited there, together, she and I; speechless, for very sorrow. In the dimming light, her face showed, shadowy—blending into the dusky mistiness that encircled us.

"Then, when a thin, curved line of soft light was all that lit the sea, she released me—pushing me from her, tenderly. Her voice sounded in my ears, 'I may not stay longer, Dear One.' It ended in a sob.

"She seemed to float away from me, and became invisible. Her voice came to me, out of the shadows, faintly; apparently from a great distance:—

" 'A little while—' It died away, remotely. In a breath, the Sea of Sleep darkened into night. Far to my left, I seemed to see, for a brief instant, a soft glow. It vanished, and, in the same moment, I became aware that I was no longer above the still sea; but once more suspended in infinite space, with the Green Sun—now eclipsed by a vast, dark sphere—before me.

"Utterly bewildered, I stared, almost unseeingly, at the ring of green flames, leaping above the dark edge. Even in the chaos of my thoughts, I wondered, dully, at their extraordinary shapes. A multitude of questions assailed me. I thought more of her, I had so lately seen, than of the sight before me. My grief, and thoughts of the future, filled me. Was I doomed to be separated from her, always? Even in the old earth-days, she had been mine, only for a little while; then she had left me, as I thought, forever. Since then, I had seen her but these times, upon the Sea of Sleep.

"A feeling of fierce resentment filled me, and miserable questionings. Why could I not have gone with my Love? What reason to keep us apart? Why had I to wait alone, while she slumbered through the years, on the still bosom of the Sea of Sleep? The Sea of Sleep! My thoughts turned, inconsequently, out of their channel of bitterness, to fresh, desperate questionings. Where was it? Where was it? I seemed to have but just parted from my Love, upon its quiet surface, and it had gone, utterly. It could not be far away! And the White Orb which I had seen hidden in the shadow of the Sun of Darkness! My sight dwelt upon the Green Sun—eclipsed. What had eclipsed it? Was there a vast, dead star circling it? Was the *Central* Sun—as I had come to regard it—a double star? The thought had come, almost unbidden; yet why should it not be so?

"My thoughts went back to the White Orb. Strange, that it should have been—I stopped. An idea had come, suddenly. The White Orb and the Green Sun! Were they one and the same? My imagination wandered backwards, and I remembered the luminous globe to which I had been so unaccountably attracted. It was curious that I should have forgotten it, even momentarily. Where were the others? I reverted again to the globe I had entered. I thought, for a time, and matters became clearer. I conceived that, by entering that impalpable globule, I had passed, at once, into some further, and, until then, invisible dimension; There, the Green Sun was still visible; but as a stupendous sphere of pale, white light—almost as though its ghost showed, and not its material part.

"A long time, I mused on the subject. I remembered how, on entering the sphere, I had, immediately, lost all sight of the others. For a still further period, I continued to revolve the different details in my mind.

"In a while, my thoughts turned to other things. I came more into the present, and began to look about me, seeingly. For the first time, I perceived that innumerable rays, of a subtle, violet hue, pierced the strange semi-darkness, in all directions. They radiated from the fiery rim of the Green Sun. They seemed to grow upon my vision, so that, in a little, I saw that they were countless. The night was filled with them—spreading outward from the Green Sun, fan-wise. I concluded that I was enabled to see them, by reason of the Sun's glory being cut off by the eclipse. They reached right out into space, and vanished.

"Gradually, as I looked, I became aware that fine points of intensely brilliant light, traversed the rays. Many of them seemed to travel from the Green Sun, into distance. Others came out of the void, towards the Sun; but one and all, each kept strictly to the ray in which it travelled. Their speed was inconceivably great; and it was only when they neared the Green Sun, or as they left it, that I could see them as separate specks of light. Further from the sun, they became thin lines of vivid fire within the violet.

"The discovery of these rays, and the moving sparks, interested me, extraordinarily. To where did they lead, in such countless profusion? I thought of the worlds in space . . . . And those sparks! Messengers! Possibly, the idea was fantastic; but I was not conscious of its being so. Messengers! Messengers from the Central Sun!

"An idea evolved itself, slowly. Was the Green Sun the abode of some vast Intelligence? The thought was bewildering. Visions of the Unnameable rose, vaguely. Had I, indeed, come upon the dwelling-place of the Eternal? For a time, I repelled the thought, dumbly. It was too stupendous. Yet . . . .

"Huge, vague thoughts had birth within me. I felt, suddenly, terribly naked. And an awful Nearness, shook me.

"And Heaven . . . ! Was that an illusion?

"My thoughts came and went, erratically. The Sea of Sleep—and she! Heaven . . . . I came back, with a bound, to the present. Somewhere, out of the void behind me, there rushed an immense, dark body—huge and silent. It was a dead star, hurling onward to the burying place of the stars. It drove between me and the Central Suns—blotting them out from my vision, and plunging me into an impenetrable night.

"An age, and I saw again the violet rays. A great while later—aeons it must have been—a circular glow grew in the sky, ahead, and I saw the edge of the receding star, show darkly against it. Thus, I knew that it was nearing the Central Suns. Presently, I saw the bright ring of the Green Sun, show plainly against the night. The star had passed into the shadow of the Dead Sun. After that, I just waited. The strange years went slowly, and ever, I watched, intently.

"The thing I had expected, came at last—suddenly, awfully. A vast flare of dazzling light. A streaming burst of white flame across the dark void. For an indefinite while, it soared outwards—a gigantic mushroom of fire. It ceased to grow. Then, as time went by, it began to sink backwards, slowly. I saw, now, that it came from a huge, glowing spot near the centre of the Dark Sun. Mighty flames, still soared outward from this. Yet, spite of its size, the grave of the star was no more than the shining of Jupiter upon the face of an ocean, when compared with the inconceivable mass of the Dead Sun.

"I may remark here, once more, that no words will ever convey to the imagination, the enormous bulk of the two Central Suns.

Chapter XXII
The Dark Nebula

"Years melted into the past, centuries, aeons. The light of the incandescent star, sank to a furious red. "It was later, that I saw the dark nebula— at first, an impalpable cloud, away to my right. It grew, steadily, to a clot of blackness in the night. How long I watched, it is impossible to say; for time, as we count it, was a thing of the past. It came closer, a shapeless monstrosity of darkness—tremendous. It seemed to slip across the night, sleepily—a very hell-fog. Slowly, it slid nearer, and passed into the void, between me and the Central Suns. It was as though a curtain had been drawn before my vision. A strange tremor of fear took me, and a fresh sense of wonder.

"The green twilight that had reigned for so many millions of years, had now given place to impenetrable gloom. Motionless, I peered about me. A century fled, and it seemed to me that I detected occasional dull glows of red, passing me at intervals.

"Earnestly, I gazed, and, presently, seemed to see circular masses, that showed muddily red, within the clouded blackness. They appeared to be growing out of the nebulous murk. Awhile, and they became plainer to my accustomed vision. I could see them, now, with a fair amount of distinctness—ruddy-tinged spheres, similar, in size, to the luminous globes that I had seen, so long previously.

"They floated past me, continually. Gradually, a peculiar uneasiness seized me. I became aware of a growing feeling of repugnance and dread. It was directed against those passing orbs, and seemed born of intuitive knowledge, rather than of any real cause or reason.

"Some of the passing globes were brighter than others; and, it was from one of these, that a face looked, suddenly. A face, human in its outline; but so tortured with woe, that I stared, aghast. I had not thought there was such sorrow, as I saw there. I was conscious of an added sense of pain, on perceiving that the eyes, which glared so wildly, were sightless. A while longer, I saw it; then it had passed on, into the surrounding gloom. After this, I saw others—all wearing that look of hopeless sorrow; and blind.

"A long time went by, and I became aware that I was nearer to the orbs, than I had been. At this, I grew uneasy; though I was less in fear of those strange globules, than I had been, before seeing their sorrowful inhabitants; for sympathy had tempered my fear.

"Later, there was no doubt but that I was being carried closer to the red spheres, and, presently, I floated among them. In awhile, I perceived one bearing down upon me. I was helpless to move from its path. In a minute, it seemed, it was upon me, and I was submerged in a deep red mist. This cleared, and I stared, confusedly, across the immense breadth of the Plain of Silence. It appeared just as I had first seen it. I was moving forward, steadily, across its surface. Away ahead, shone the vast, blood-red ring* that lit the place. All around, was spread the extraordinary desolation of stillness, that had so impressed me during my previous wanderings across its starkness.

* Without doubt, the flame-edged mass of the Dead Central Sun, seen from another dimension.—Ed.

"Presently, I saw, rising up into the ruddy gloom, the distant peaks of the mighty amphitheatre of mountains, where, untold ages before, I had been shown my first glimpse of the terrors that underlie many things; and where, vast and silent, watched by a thousand mute gods, stands the replica of this house of mysteries—this house that I had seen swallowed up in that hell-fire, ere the earth had kissed the sun, and vanished for ever.

"Though I could see the crests of the mountain-amphitheatre, yet it was a great while before their lower portions became visible. Possibly, this was due to the strange, ruddy haze, that seemed to cling to the surface of the Plain. However, be this as it may, I saw them at last.

"In a still further space of time, I had come so close to the mountains, that they appeared to overhang me. Presently, I saw the great rift, open before me, and I drifted into it; without volition on my part.

"Later, I came out upon the breadth of the enormous arena. There, at an apparent distance of some five miles, stood the House, huge, monstrous and silent—lying in the very centre of that stupendous amphitheatre. So far as I could see, it had not altered in any way; but looked as though it were only yesterday that I had seen it. Around, the grim, dark mountains frowned down upon me from their lofty silences.

"Far to my right, away up among inaccessible peaks, loomed the enormous bulk of the great Beast-god. Higher, I saw the hideous form of the dread goddess, rising up through the red gloom, thousands of fathoms above me. To the left, I made out the monstrous Eyeless-Thing, grey and inscrutable. Further off, reclining on its lofty ledge, the livid Ghoul-Shape showed—a splash of sinister colour, among the dark mountains.

"Slowly, I moved out across the great arena—floating. As I went, I made out the dim forms of many of the other lurking Horrors that peopled those supreme heights.

"Gradually, I neared the House, and my thoughts flashed back across the abyss of years. I remembered the dread Spectre of the Place. A short while passed, and I saw that I was being wafted directly towards the enormous mass of that silent building.

"About this time, I became aware, in an indifferent sort of way, of a growing sense of numbness, that robbed me of the fear, which I should otherwise have felt, on approaching that awesome Pile. As it was, I viewed it, calmly—much as a man views calamity through the haze of his tobacco smoke.

"In a little while, I had come so close to the House, as to be able to distinguish many of the details about it. The longer I looked, the more was I confirmed in my long-ago impressions of its entire similitude to this strange house. Save in its enormous size, I could find nothing unlike.

"Suddenly, as I stared, a great feeling of amazement filled me. I had come opposite to that part, where the outer door, leading into the study, is situated. There, lying right across the threshold, lay a great length of coping stone, identical—save in size and colour—with the piece I had dislodged in my fight with the Pit-creatures.

"I floated nearer, and my astonishment increased, as I noted that the door was broken partly from its hinges, precisely in the manner that my study door had been forced inwards, by the assaults of the Swine-things. The sight started a train of thoughts, and I began to trace, dimly, that the attack on this house, might have a far deeper significance than I had, hitherto, imagined. I remembered how, long ago, in the old earth-days, I had half suspected that, in some unexplainable manner, this house, in which I live, was *en rapport*—to use a recognised term—with that other tremendous structure, away in the midst of that incomparable Plain.

"Now, however, it began to be borne upon me, that I had but vaguely conceived what the realisation of my suspicion meant. I began to understand, with a more than human clearness, that the attack I had repelled, was, in some extraordinary manner, connected with an attack upon that strange edifice.

"With a curious inconsequence, my thoughts abruptly left the matter; to dwell, wonderingly, upon the peculiar material, out of which the House was constructed. It was—as I have mentioned, earlier—of a deep, green colour. Yet, now that I had come so close to it, I perceived that it fluctuated at times, though slightly—glowing and fading, much as do the fumes of phosphorus, when rubbed upon the hand, in the dark.

"Presently, my attention was distracted from this, by coming to the great entrance. Here, for the first time, I was afraid; for, all in a moment, the huge doors swung back, and I drifted in between them, helplessly. Inside, all was blackness, impalpable. In an instant, I had crossed the threshold, and the great doors closed, silently, shutting me in that lightless place.

"For a while, I seemed to hang, motionless; suspended amid the darkness. Then, I became conscious that I was moving again; where, I could not tell. Suddenly, far down beneath me, I seemed to hear a murmurous noise of Swine-laughter. It sank away, and the succeeding silence appeared clogged with horror.

"Then a door opened somewhere ahead; a white haze of light filtered through, and I floated slowly into a room, that seemed strangely familiar. All at once, there came a bewildering, screaming noise, that deafened me. I saw a blurred vista of visions, flaming before my sight. My senses were dazed, through the space of an eternal moment. Then, my power of seeing, came back to me. The dizzy, hazy feeling passed, and I saw, clearly.

Chapter XXIII
Pepper

"I was seated in my chair, back again in this old study. My glance wandered round the room. For a minute, it had a strange, quivery appearance—unreal and unsubstantial. This disappeared, and I saw that nothing was altered in any way. I looked towards the end window—the blind was up.

"I rose to my feet, shakily. As I did so, a slight noise, in the direction of the door, attracted my attention. I glanced towards it. For a short instant, it appeared to me that it was being closed, gently. I stared, and saw that I must have been mistaken—it seemed closely shut.

"With a succession of efforts, I trod my way to the window, and looked out. The sun was just rising, lighting up the tangled wilderness of gardens. For, perhaps, a minute, I stood, and stared. I passed my hand, confusedly, across my forehead.

"Presently, amid the chaos of my senses, a sudden thought came to me; I turned, quickly, and called to Pepper. There was no answer, and I stumbled across the room, in a quick access of fear. As I went, I tried to frame his name; but my lips were numb. I reached the table, and stooped down to him, with a catching at my heart. He was lying in the shadow of the table, and I had not been able to see him, distinctly, from the window. Now, as I stooped, I took my breath, shortly. There was no Pepper; instead, I was reaching towards an elongated, little heap of grey, ash-like dust . . . .

"I must have remained, in that half-stooped position, for some minutes. I was dazed—stunned. Pepper had really passed into the land of shadows.

Chapter XXIV
The Footsteps in the Garden

"Pepper is dead! Even now, at times, I seem scarcely able to realise that this is so. It is many weeks, since I came back from that strange and terrible journey through space and time. Sometimes, in my sleep, I dream about it, and go through, in imagination, the whole of that fearsome happening. When I wake, my thoughts dwell upon it. That Sun—those Suns, were they indeed the great Central Suns, round which the whole universe, of the unknown heavens, revolves? Who shall say? And the bright globules, floating forever in the light of the Green Sun! And the Sea of Sleep on which they float! How unbelievable it all is. If it were not for Pepper, I should, even after the many extraordinary things that I have witnessed, be inclined to imagine that it was but a gigantic dream. Then, there is that dreadful, dark nebula (with its multitudes of red spheres) moving always within the shadow of the Dark Sun, sweeping along on its stupendous orbit, wrapped eternally in gloom. And the faces that peered out at me! God, do they, and does such a thing really exist? . . . There is still that little heap of grey ash, on my study floor. I will not have it touched.

"At times, when I am calmer, I have wondered what became of the outer planets of the Solar System. It has occurred to me, that they may have broken loose from the sun's attraction, and whirled away into space. This is, of course, only a surmise. There are so many things, about which I wonder.

"Now that I am writing, let me record that I am certain, there is something horrible about to happen. Last night, a thing occurred, which has filled me with an even greater terror, than did the Pit fear. I will write it down now, and, if anything more happens, endeavour to make a note of it, at once. I have a feeling, that there is more in this last affair, than in all those others. I am shaky and nervous, even now, as I write. Somehow, I think death is not very far away. Not that I fear death—as death is understood. Yet, there is that in the air, which bids me fear—an intangible, cold horror. I felt it last night. It was thus:—

"Last night, I was sitting here in my study, writing. The door, leading into the garden, was half open. At times, the metallic rattle of a dog's chain, sounded faintly. It belongs to the dog I have bought, since Pepper's death. I will not have him in the house—not after Pepper. Still, I have felt it better to have a dog about the place. They are wonderful creatures.

"I was much engrossed in my work, and the time passed, quickly. Suddenly, I heard a soft noise on the path, outside in the garden—pad, pad, pad, it went, with a stealthy, curious sound. I sat upright, with a quick movement, and looked out through the opened door. Again the noise came—pad, pad, pad. It appeared to be approaching. With a slight feeling of nervousness, I stared into the gardens; but the night hid everything.

"Then the dog gave a long howl, and I started. For a minute, perhaps, I peered, intently; but could hear nothing. After a little, I picked up the pen, which I had laid down, and recommenced my work. The nervous feeling had gone; for I imagined that the sound I had heard, was nothing more than the dog walking round his kennel, at the length of his chain.

"A quarter of an hour may have passed; then, all at once, the dog howled again, and with such a plaintively sorrowful note, that I jumped to my feet, dropping my pen, and inking the page on which I was at work.

" 'Curse that dog!' I muttered, noting what I had done. Then, even as I said the words, there sounded again that queer—pad, pad, pad. It was horribly close—almost by the door, I thought. I knew, now, that it could not be the dog; his chain would not allow him to come so near.

"The dog's growl came again, and I noted, subconsciously, the taint of fear in it.

"Outside, on the windowsill, I could see Tip, my sister's pet cat. As I looked, it sprang to its feet, its tail swelling, visibly. For an instant it stood thus; seeming to stare, fixedly, at something, in the direction of the door. Then, quickly, it began to back along the sill; until, reaching the wall at the end, it could go no further. There it stood, rigid, as though frozen in an attitude of extraordinary terror.

"Frightened, and puzzled, I seized a stick from the corner, and went towards the door, silently; taking one of the candles with me. I had come to within a few paces of it, when, suddenly, a peculiar sense of fear thrilled through me—a fear, palpitant and real; whence, I knew not, nor why. So great was the feeling of terror, that I wasted no time; but retreated straight-way—walking backwards, and keeping my gaze, fearfully, on the door. I would have given much, to rush at it, fling it to, and shoot the bolts; for I have had it repaired and strengthened, so that, now, it is far stronger than ever it has been. Like Tip, I continued my, almost unconscious, progress backwards, until the wall brought me up. At that, I started, nervously, and glanced round, apprehensively. As I did so, my eyes dwelt, momentarily, on the rack of firearms, and I took a step towards them; but stopped, with a curious feeling that they would be needless. Outside, in the gardens, the dog moaned, strangely.

"Suddenly, from the cat, there came a fierce, long screech. I glanced, jerkily, in its direction—Something, luminous and ghostly, encircled it, and grew upon my vision. It resolved into a glowing hand, transparent, with a lambent, greenish flame flickering over it. The cat gave a last, awful caterwaul, and I saw it smoke and blaze. My breath came with a gasp, and I leant against the wall. Over that part of the window there spread a smudge, green and fantastic. It hid the thing from me, though the glare of fire shone through, dully. A stench of burning, stole into the room.

"Pad, pad, pad—Something passed down the garden path, and a faint, mouldy odour seemed to come in through the open door, and mingle with the burnt smell.

"The dog had been silent for a few moments. Now, I heard him yowl, sharply, as though in pain. Then, he was quiet, save for an occasional, subdued whimper of fear.

"A minute went by; then the gate on the West side of the gardens, slammed, distantly. After that, nothing; not even the dog's whine.

"I must have stood there some minutes. Then a fragment of courage stole into my heart, and I made a frightened rush at the door, dashed it to, and bolted it. After that, for a full half-hour, I sat, helpless—staring before me, rigidly.

"Slowly, my life came back into me, and I made my way, shakily, up-stairs to bed.

"That is all.

Chapter XXV
The Thing from the Arena

"This morning, early, I went through the gardens; but found everything as usual. Near the door, I examined the path, for footprints; yet, here again, there was nothing to tell me whether, or not, I dreamed last night.

"It was only when I came to speak to the dog, that I discovered tangible proof, that something did happen. When I went to his kennel, he kept inside, crouching up in one corner, and I had to coax him, to get him out. When, finally, he consented to come, it was in a strangely cowed and subdued manner. As I patted him, my attention was attracted to a greenish patch, on his left flank. On examining it, I found, that the fur and skin had been apparently, burnt off; for the flesh showed, raw and scorched. The shape of the mark was curious, reminding me of the imprint of a large talon or hand.

"I stood up, thoughtful. My gaze wandered towards the study window. The rays of the rising sun, shimmered on the smoky patch in the lower corner, causing it to fluctuate from green to red, oddly. Ah! that was undoubtedly another proof; and, suddenly, the horrible Thing I saw last night, rose in my mind. I looked at the dog, again. I knew the cause, now, of that hateful looking wound on his side—I knew, also, that, what I had seen last night, had been a real happening. And a great discomfort filled me. Pepper! Tip! And now this poor animal . . . ! I glanced at the dog again, and noticed that he was licking at his wound.

" 'Poor brute!' I muttered, and bent to pat his head. At that, he got upon his feet, nosing and licking my hand, wistfully.

"Presently, I left him, having other matters to which to attend.

"After dinner, I went to see him, again. He seemed quiet, and disinclined to leave his kennel. From my sister, I have learnt that he has refused all food today. She appeared a little puzzled, when she told me; though quite unsuspicious of anything of which to be afraid.

"The day has passed, uneventfully enough. After tea, I went, again, to have a look at the dog. He seemed moody, and somewhat restless; yet persisted in remaining in his kennel. Before locking up, for the night, I moved his kennel out, away from the wall, so that I shall be able to watch it from the small window, tonight. The thought came to me, to bring him into the house for the night; but consideration has decided me, to let him remain out. I cannot say that the house is, in any degree, less to be feared than the gardens. Pepper was in the house, and yet . . . .

"It is now two o'clock. Since eight, I have watched the kennel, from the small, side window in my study. Yet, nothing has occurred, and I am too tired to watch longer. I will go to bed . . . .

"During the night, I was restless. This is unusual for me; but, towards morning, I obtained a few hours' sleep.

"I rose early, and, after breakfast, visited the dog. He was quiet; but morose, and refused to leave his kennel. I wish there was some horse doctor near here; I would have the poor brute looked to. All day, he has taken no food; but has shown an evident desire for water—lapping it up, greedily. I was relieved to observe this.

"The evening has come, and I am in my study. I intend to follow my plan of last night, and watch the kennel. The door, leading into the garden, is bolted, securely. I am consciously glad there are bars to the windows . . . .

"Night:—Midnight has gone. The dog has been silent, up to the present. Through the side window, on my left, I can make out, dimly, the outlines of the kennel. For the first time, the dog moves, and I hear the rattle of his chain. I look out, quickly. As I stare, the dog moves again, restlessly, and I see a small patch of luminous light, shine from the interior of the kennel. It vanishes; then the dog stirs again, and, once more, the gleam comes. I am puzzled. The dog is quiet, and I can see the luminous thing, plainly. It shows distinctly. There is something familiar about the shape of it. For a moment, I wonder; then it comes to me, that it is not unlike the four fingers and thumb of a hand. Like a hand! And I remember the contour of that fearsome wound on the dog's side. It must be the wound I see. It is luminous at night—Why? The minutes pass. My mind is filled with this fresh thing . . . .

"Suddenly, I hear a sound, out in the gardens. How it thrills through me. It is approaching. Pad, pad, pad. A prickly sensation traverses my spine, and seems to creep across my scalp. The dog moves in his kennel, and whimpers, frightenedly. He must have turned round; for, now, I can no longer see the outline of his shining wound.

"Outside, the gardens are silent, once more, and I listen, fearfully. A minute passes, and another; then I hear the padding sound, again. It is quite close, and appears to be coming down the gravelled path. The noise is curiously measured and deliberate. It ceases outside the door; and I rise to my feet, and stand motionless. From the door, comes a slight sound—the latch is being slowly raised. A singing noise is in my ears, and I have a sense of pressure about the head—

"The latch drops, with a sharp click, into the catch. The noise startles me afresh; jarring, horribly, on my tense nerves. After that, I stand, for a long while, amid an ever-growing quietness. All at once, my knees begin to tremble, and I have to sit, quickly.

"An uncertain period of time passes, and, gradually, I begin to shake off the feeling of terror, that has possessed me. Yet, still I sit. I seem to have lost the power of movement. I am strangely tired, and inclined to doze. My eyes open and close, and, presently, I find myself falling asleep, and waking, in fits and starts.

"It is some time later, that I am sleepily aware that one of the candles is guttering. When I wake again, it has gone out, and the room is very dim, under the light of the one remaining flame. The semi-darkness troubles me little. I have lost that awful sense of dread, and my only desire seems to be to sleep—sleep.

"Suddenly, although there is no noise, I am awake—wide awake. I am acutely conscious of the nearness of some mystery, of some overwhelming Presence. The very air seems pregnant with terror. I sit huddled, and just listen, intently. Still, there is no sound. Nature, herself, seems dead. Then, the oppressive stillness is broken by a little eldritch scream of wind, that sweeps round the house, and dies away, remotely.

"I let my gaze wander across the half-lighted room. By the great clock in the far corner, is a dark, tall shadow. For a short instant, I stare, frightenedly. Then, I see that it is nothing, and am, momentarily, relieved.

"In the time that follows, the thought flashes through my brain, why not leave this house—this house of mystery and terror? Then, as though in answer, there sweeps up, across my sight, a vision of the wondrous Sea of Sleep,—the Sea of Sleep where she and I have been allowed to meet, after the years of separation and sorrow; and I know that I shall stay on here, whatever happens.

"Through the side window, I note the sombre blackness of the night. My glance wanders away, and round the room; resting on one shadowy object and another. Suddenly, I turn, and look at the window on my right; as I do so, I breathe quickly, and bend forward, with a frightened gaze at something outside the window, but close to the bars. I am looking at a vast, misty swine-face, over which fluctuates a flamboyant flame, of a greenish hue. It is the Thing from the arena. The quivering mouth seems to drip with a continual, phosphorescent slaver. The eyes are staring straight into the room, with an inscrutable expression. Thus, I sit rigidly—frozen.

"The Thing has begun to move. It is turning, slowly, in my direction. Its face is coming round towards me. It sees me. Two huge, inhumanly human, eyes are looking through the dimness at me. I am cold with fear; yet, even now, I am keenly conscious, and note, in an irrelevant way, that the distant stars are blotted out by the mass of the giant face.

"A fresh horror has come to me. I am rising from my chair, without the least intention. I am on my feet, and something is impelling me towards the door that leads out into the gardens. I wish to stop; but cannot. Some immutable power is opposed to my will, and I go slowly forward, unwilling and resistant. My glance flies round the room, helplessly, and stops at the window. The great swine-face has disappeared, and I hear, again, that stealthy pad, pad, pad. It stops outside the door—the door towards which I am being compelled . . . .

"There succeeds a short, intense silence; then there comes a sound. It is the rattle of the latch, being slowly lifted. At that, I am filled with desperation. I will not go forward another step. I make a vast effort to return; but it

is, as though I press back, upon an invisible wall. I groan out loud, in the agony of my fear, and the sound of my voice is frightening. Again comes that rattle, and I shiver, clammily. I try—aye, fight and struggle, to hold back, *back*; but it is no use . . . .

"I am at the door, and, in a mechanical way, I watch my hand go forward, to undo the topmost bolt. It does so, entirely without my volition. Even as I reach up towards the bolt, the door is violently shaken, and I get a sickly whiff of mouldy air, which seems to drive in through the interstices of the doorway. I draw the bolt back, slowly, fighting, dumbly, the while. It comes out of its socket, with a click, and I begin to shake, aguishly. There are two more; one at the bottom of the door; the other, a massive affair, is placed about the middle.

"For, perhaps a minute, I stand, with my arms hanging slackly, by my sides. The influence to meddle with the fastenings of the door, seems to have gone. All at once, there comes the sudden rattle of iron, at my feet. I glance down, quickly, and realise, with an unspeakable terror, that my foot is pushing back the lower bolt. An awful sense of helplessness assails me . . . . The bolt comes out of its hold, with a slight, ringing sound and I stagger on my feet, grasping at the great, central bolt, for support. A minute passes, an eternity; then another—My God, help me! I am being forced to work upon the last fastening. *I will not!* Better to die, than open to the Terror, that is on the other side of the door. Is there no escape . . . ? God help me, I have jerked the bolt half out of its socket! My lips emit a hoarse scream of terror, the bolt is three parts drawn, now, and still my unconscious hands work towards my doom. Only a fraction of steel, between my soul and That. Twice, I scream out in the supreme agony of my fear; then, with a mad effort, I tear my hands away. My eyes seem blinded.

A great blackness is falling upon me. Nature has come to my rescue. I feel my knees giving. There is a loud, quick thudding upon the door, and I am falling, falling . . . .

"I must have lain there, at least a couple of hours. As I recover, I am aware that the other candle has burnt out, and the room is in an almost total darkness. I cannot rise to my feet, for I am cold, and filled with a terrible cramp. Yet my brain is clear, and there is no longer the strain of that unholy influence.

"Cautiously, I get upon my knees, and feel for the central bolt. I find it, and push it securely back into its socket; then the one at the bottom of the door. By this time, I am able to rise to my feet, and so manage to secure the fastening at the top. After that, I go down upon my knees, again, and creep away among the furniture, in the direction of the stairs. By doing this, I am safe from observation from the window.

"I reach the opposite door, and, as I leave the study, cast one nervous glance over my shoulder, towards the window. Out in the night, I seem to catch a glimpse of something impalpable; but it may be only a fancy. Then, I am in the passage, and on the stairs.

"Reaching my bedroom, I clamber into bed, all clothed as I am, and pull the bedclothes over me. There, after a while, I begin to regain a little confidence. It is impossible to sleep; but I am grateful for the added warmth of the bedclothes. Presently, I try to think over the happenings of the past night; but, though I cannot sleep, I find that it is useless, to attempt consecutive thought. My brain seems curiously blank.

"Towards morning, I begin to toss, uneasily. I cannot rest, and, after a while, I get out of bed, and pace the floor. The wintry dawn is beginning to creep through the windows, and shows the bare discomfort of the old room. Strange, that, through all these years, it has never occurred to me how dismal the place really is. And so a time passes.

"From somewhere down stairs, a sound comes up to me. I go to the bedroom door, and listen. It is Mary, bustling about the great, old kitchen, getting the breakfast ready. I feel little interest. I am not hungry. My thoughts, however; continue to dwell upon her. How little the weird happenings in this house seem to trouble her. Except in the incident of the Pit creatures, she has seemed unconscious of anything unusual occurring. She is old, like myself; yet how little we have to do with one another. Is it because we have nothing in common; or only that, being old, we care less for society, than quietness? These and other matters pass through my mind, as I meditate; and help to distract my attention, for a while, from the oppressive thoughts of the night.

"After a time, I go to the window, and, opening it, look out. The sun is now above the horizon, and the air, though cold, is sweet and crisp. Gradually, my brain clears, and a sense of security, for the time being, comes to me. Somewhat happier, I go down stairs, and out into the garden, to have a look at the dog.

"As I approach the kennel, I am greeted by the same mouldy stench that assailed me at the door last night. Shaking off a momentary sense of fear, I call to the dog; but he takes no heed, and, after calling once more, I throw a small stone into the kennel. At this, he moves, uneasily, and I shout his name, again; but do not go closer. Presently, my sister comes out, and joins me, in trying to coax him from the kennel.

"In a little the poor beast rises, and shambles out lurching queerly. In the daylight he stands swaying from side to side, and blinking stupidly. I look and note that the horrid wound is larger, much larger, and seems to have a whitish, fungoid appearance. My sister moves to fondle him; but I detain her, and explain that I think it will be better not to go too near him for a few days; as it is impossible to tell what may be the matter with him; and it is well to be cautious.

"A minute later, she leaves me; coming back with a basin of odd scraps of food. This she places on the ground, near the dog, and I push it into his reach, with the aid of a branch, broken from one of the shrubs. Yet, though the meat should be tempting, he takes no notice of it; but retires to his kennel. There is still water in his drinking vessel, so, after a few moments' talk, we go back to the house. I can see that my sister is much puzzled as to what is the matter with the animal; yet it would be madness, even to hint the truth to her.

"The day slips away, uneventfully; and night comes on. I have determined to repeat my experiment of last night. I cannot say that it is wisdom; yet my mind is made up. Still, however, I have taken precautions; for I have driven stout nails in at the back of each of the three bolts, that secure the door, opening from the study into the gardens. This will, at least, prevent a recurrence of the danger I ran last night.

"From ten to about two-thirty, I watch; but nothing occurs; and, finally, I stumble off to bed, where I am soon asleep.

Chapter XXVI

The Luminous Speck

" I awake suddenly. It is still dark. I turn over, once or twice, in my endeavours to sleep again; but I cannot sleep. My head is aching, slightly; and, by turns I am hot and cold. In a little, I give up the attempt, and stretch out my hand, for the matches. I will light my candle, and read, awhile; perhaps, I shall be able to sleep, after a time. For a few moments, I grope; then my hand touches the box; but, as I open it, I am startled, to see a phosphorescent speck of fire, shining amid the darkness. I put out my other hand, and touch it. It is on my wrist. With a feeling of vague alarm, I strike a light, hurriedly, and look; but can see nothing, save a tiny scratch.

" 'Fancy!' I mutter, with a half sigh of relief. Then the match burns my finger, and I drop it, quickly. As I fumble for another, the thing shines out again. I know, now, that it is no fancy. This time, I light the candle, and examine the place, more closely. There is a slight, greenish discolouration round the scratch. I am puzzled and worried. Then a thought comes to me. I remember the morning after the Thing appeared. I remember that the dog licked my hand. It was this one, with the scratch on it; though I have not been even conscious of the abrasement, until now. A horrible fear has come to me. It creeps into my brain—the dog's wound, shines at night. With a dazed feeling, I sit down on the side of the bed, and try to think; but cannot. My brain seems numbed with the sheer horror of this new fear.

"Time moves on, unheeded. Once, I rouse up, and try to persuade myself that I am mistaken; but it is no use. In my heart, I have no doubt.

"Hour after hour, I sit in the darkness and silence, and shiver, hopelessly . . . .

"The day has come and gone, and it is night again.

"This morning, early, I shot the dog, and buried it, away among the bushes. My sister is startled and frightened; but I am desperate. Besides, it is better so. The foul growth had almost hidden its left side. And I—the place on my wrist has enlarged, perceptibly. Several times, I have caught myself muttering prayers—little things learnt as a child. God, Almighty God, help me! I shall go mad.

"Six days, and I have eaten nothing. It is night. I am sitting in my chair. Ah, God! I wonder have any ever felt the horror of life that I have come to know? I am swathed in terror. I feel ever the burning of this dread growth. It has covered all my right arm and side, and is beginning to creep up my neck. Tomorrow, it will eat into my face. I shall become a terrible mass of living corruption. There is no escape. Yet, a thought has come to me, born of a sight of the gun-rack, on the other side of the room. I have looked again—with the strangest of feelings. The thought grows upon me. God, Thou knowest, Thou must know, that death is better, aye, better a thousand times than This. This! Jesus, forgive me, but I cannot live, cannot, cannot! I dare not! I am beyond all help—there is nothing else left. It will, at least, spare me that final horror . . . .

"I think I must have been dozing. I am very weak, and oh! so miserable, so miserable and tired—tired. The rustle of the paper, tries my brain. My hearing seems preternaturally sharp. I will sit awhile and think . . . .

"Hush! I hear something, down—down in the cellars. It is a creaking sound. My God, it is the opening of the great, oak trap. What can be doing that? The scratching of my pen deafens me . . . I must listen . . . . There are steps on the stairs; strange padding steps, that come up and nearer . . . . Jesus, be merciful to me, an old man. There is something fumbling at the door-handle. O God, help me now! Jesus—The door is opening—slowly. Somethi—"

That is all.

NOTE.—From the unfinished word, it is possible, on the MS., to trace a faint line of ink, which suggests that the pen has trailed away over the paper; possibly, through fright and weakness.—Ed.

Chapter XXVII
Conclusion

I put down the Manuscript, and glanced across at Tonnison: he was sitting, staring out into the dark. I waited a minute; then I spoke.

"Well?" I said.

He turned, slowly, and looked at me. His thoughts seemed to have gone out of him into a great distance.

"Was he mad?" I asked, and indicated the MS., with a half nod.

Tonnison stared at me, unseeingly, a moment; then, his wits came back to him, and, suddenly, he comprehended my question.

"No!" he said.

I opened my lips, to offer a contradictory opinion; for my sense of the saneness of things, would not allow me to take the story literally; then I shut them again, without saying anything. Somehow, the certainty in Tonnison's voice affected my doubts. I felt, all at once, less assured; though I was by no means convinced as yet.

After a few moments' silence, Tonnison rose, stiffly, and began to undress. He seemed disinclined to talk; so I said nothing; but followed his example. I was weary; though still full of the story I had just read.

Somehow, as I rolled into my blankets, there crept into my mind a memory of the old gardens, as we had seen them.

I remembered the odd fear that the place had conjured up in our hearts; and it grew upon me, with conviction, that Tonnison was right.

It was very late when we rose—nearly midday; for the greater part of the night had been spent in reading the MS.

Tonnison was grumpy, and I felt out of sorts. It was a somewhat dismal day, and there was a touch of chilliness in the air. There was no mention of going out fishing on either of our parts. We got dinner, and, after that, just sat and smoked in silence.

Presently, Tonnison asked for the Manuscript: I handed it to him, and he spent most of the afternoon in reading it through by himself.

It was while he was thus employed, that a thought came to me:—

"What do you say to having another look at—?" I nodded my head down stream.

Tonnison looked up. "Nothing!" he said, abruptly; and, somehow, I was less annoyed, than relieved, at his answer.

After that, I left him alone.

A little before teatime, he looked up at me, curiously.

"Sorry, old chap, if I was a bit short with you just now;" (just now, indeed! he had not spoken for the last three hours) "but I would not go there again," and he indicated with his head, "for anything that you could offer me. Ugh!" and he put down that history of a man's terror and hope and despair.

The next morning, we rose early, and went for our accustomed swim: we had partly shaken off the depression of the previous day; and so, took our rods when we had finished breakfast, and spent the day at our favourite sport.

After that day, we enjoyed our holiday to the utmost; though both of us looked forward to the time when our driver should come; for we were tremendously anxious to inquire of him, and through him among the people of the tiny hamlet, whether any of them could give us information about that strange garden, lying away by itself in the heart of an almost unknown tract of country.

At last, the day came, on which we expected the driver to come across for us. He arrived early, while we were still abed; and, the first thing we knew, he was at the opening of the tent, inquiring whether we had had good sport. We replied in the affirmative; and then, both together, almost in the same breath, we asked the question that was uppermost in our minds:—Did he know anything about an old garden, and a great pit, and a lake, situated some miles away, down the river; also, had he ever heard of a great house thereabouts?

No, he did not, and had not; yet, stay, he had heard a rumour, once upon a time, of a great, old house standing alone out in the wilderness; but, if he remembered rightly it was a place given over to the fairies; or, if that had not been so, he was certain that there had been something "quare" about it; and, anyway, he had heard nothing of it for a very long while—not since he was quite a gossoon. No, he could not remember anything particular about it; indeed, he did not know he remembered anything "at all, at all" until we questioned him.

"Look here," said Tonnison, finding that this was about all that he could tell us, "just take a walk round the village, while we dress, and find out something, if you can."

With a nondescript salute, the man departed on his errand; while we made haste to get into our clothes; after which, we began to prepare breakfast.

We were just sitting down to it, when he returned.

"It's all in bed the lazy divvils is, sor," he said, with a repetition of the salute, and an appreciative eye to the good things spread out on our provision chest, which we utilised as a table.

"Oh, well, sit down," replied my friend, "and have something to eat with us." Which the man did without delay.

After breakfast, Tonnison sent him off again on the same errand, while we sat and smoked. He was away some three-quarters of an hour, and, when he returned, it was evident that he had found out something. It appeared that he had got into conversation with an ancient man of the village, who, probably, knew more—though it was little enough—of the strange house, than any other person living.

The substance of this knowledge was, that, in the "ancient man's" youth—and goodness knows how long back that was—there had stood a great house in the centre of the gardens, where now was left only that fragment of ruin. This house had been empty for a great while; years before his—the ancient man's—birth. It was a place shunned by the people of the village, as it had been shunned by their fathers before them. There were many things said about it, and all were of evil. No one ever went near it, either by day or night. In the village it was a synonym of all that is unholy and dreadful.

And then, one day, a man, a stranger, had ridden through the village, and turned off down the river, in the direction of the House, as it was always termed by the villagers. Some hours afterwards, he had ridden back, taking the track by which he had come, towards Ardrahan. Then, for three months or so, nothing was heard. At the end of that time, he reappeared; but now, he was accompanied by an elderly woman, and a large number of donkeys, laden with various articles. They had passed through the village without stopping, and gone straight down the bank of the river, in the direction of the House.

Since that time, no one, save the man whom they had chartered to bring over monthly supplies of necessaries from Ardrahan, had ever seen either of them: and him, none had ever induced to talk; evidently, he had been well paid for his trouble.

The years had moved onward, uneventfully enough, in that little hamlet; the man making his monthly journeys, regularly.

One day, he had appeared as usual on his customary errand. He had passed through the village without exchanging more than a surly nod with the inhabitants and gone on towards the House. Usually, it was evening before he made the return journey. On this occasion, however, he had reappeared in the village, a few hours later, in an extraordinary state of excitement, and with the astounding information, that the House had disappeared bodily, and that a stupendous pit now yawned in the place where it had stood.

This news, it appears, so excited the curiosity of the villagers, that they overcame their fears, and marched *en masse* to the place. There, they found everything, just as described by the carrier.

This was all that we could learn. Of the author of the MS., who he was, and whence he came, we shall never know.

His identity is, as he seems to have desired, buried forever.

That same day, we left the lonely village of Kraighten. We have never been there since.

Sometimes, in my dreams, I see that enormous pit, surrounded, as it is, on all sides by wild trees and bushes. And the noise of the water rises upwards, and blends—in my sleep—with other and lower noises; while, over all, hangs the eternal shroud of spray.

An Aberrant Afterword:
Blowing Dust in the House of Incest

"It might have been a million years later." Who could be heartless enough to resist the innocent hubris of that opening to Chapter XVII of William Hope Hodgson's *The House on the Borderland*, which caught my eye as I beachcombed, one Saturday morning in the late Sixties, among the unpurged slag of Kingsland Waste market? We were dealing then in shillings and pence. And old Jock, the sadly-missed bibliophile and journeyman pornographer, was about to paste his inevitable 3d sticker to the top right-hand corner of the captive volume. I wrestled it from his arthritic grip. I confess: I was already hooked.

The version I had so casually adopted (title in blush-pink on a slippery silver background) was a 1969 reissue by Panther. Alan Aldridge, the famous-for-being-famous Penguin revivalist, had been brought in to provide the hook: a shockingly inappropriate funhouse cartoon. The sort of tattoo you know you're going to regret in the morning. The book looked like a detail torn from the hoarding of a projected Roger Corman theme-park. But the timing of the release was preternaturally sharp.

This startling and heterodox fantasy, originally published in 1908, was ripe for targeting, sixty years later, at the grandchildren of Aldous Huxley, the kissing-cousins of Castaneda. Hodgson's transcendent visions of Heaven and

Hell convinced us, in the authenticity of their depiction, to enter a narcotic world, with its own laws of physics, its rigorous exclusion of unnecessary data: an ungoverned principality on the "borders of the Silences". We have, not so much to suspend our disbelief, as to accept an involuntary implication in a genetic chain of unravelling horrors: to become participants, rather than spectators. The age of the brutalized voyeur, with his cache of electronic gewgaws, was still ahead of us. It was a characteristic of the misunderstood and scapegoat decade in which I made the book's acquaintance that our voyages to the extremities of time and space were launched from familiar ground. It was a common creed that the ordinary should open its doors upon the marvellous. *The House on the Borderland* could be touted, shamelessly, as a "pre-psychedelic trip". You could share the exhilaration of disintegrating egoic consciousness—without the pain, without the tedious years of meditation and struggle.

So this was heavy stuff—to be as incontinently (mis)construed as the coda to Stanley Kubrick's and Arthur C. Clarke's *2001: A Space Odyssey*, which arrived in our cinemas at about the same time. Freakish out-of-the-body experiences were tellingly cut against the sneak assaults of phosphorus-drooling "swine creatures" going heroically over the top in the hope of being noticed by Hunter S. Thompson.

But *The House on the Borderland*, as with any enduring work of fiction, survives the polemical "interpretations" of one generation. The singular quality of the narrative is cloaked within a deceptively simple structure. Hodgson reminds us, before we begin, that "the inner story must be uncovered, personally, by each reader, according to ability and desire". He provides the clues, hints, moments of self-revelation that rise proud from the plain course allotted to them.

The author/editor has accepted responsibility for a curious antiquarian manuscript, "a small book . . . filled with a quaint but legible hand-writing." Just how he won possession of it, he does not choose to inform us. The nuclear heart of the tale is further distanced by the journalistic intervention of two Englishmen, travelling through the West of Ireland, enjoying a leisurely and indirected "vacation"—from what, or from where, is not disclosed. The queerness of their names, Tonnison and Berreggnog, sounding so much like anagrams, persuades me to propose a Theological College in the eastern counties.

These muscular Christians present themselves in the guise of sportsmen in quest of some decent angling, nothing more. We are instantly alerted. We have been here before. They are obviously suspect, straight out of stock. In a thriller by John Buchan they would stumble across nothing more unpleasant that an alien conspiracy to rot the moral fibre of the Empire. In a film by Alfred Hitchcock they would be unmasked by some quirky detail, fishing for trout in a septic tank, revealing themselves as conspirators, the League of the Friends of the Mule-Footed Hog. Their role in this affair is, I'm afraid, deeply ambiguous. It has no real purpose, other than to lay down a little local colour, and then lead us directly to the "crumpled and dilapidated" notebook, once hidden among the ruins of an ancient house, but now resting securely in the hands of William Hope Hodgson of Borth.

Is it the Recluse's holograph journal that Hodgson now subjects to "a swift, jerky examination"—surely an odd description this, hinting at the onanistic seizure of the hardcore collector—or is it the full printed text of *The House on the Borderland*, with its framing device and account of the discovery of the manuscript? If the editor is contemplating the finished version, was it Berreggnog who "handed it" to him? And under what circumstances? As a gift, or a curse?

Is the whole edifice of author, travellers, picturesque detail, a cover story to make bearable the incandescent ecstasies of the visions and nightmares? In their naked form they would read like the ravings of a mystic or a drug-fiend. Even De Quincey needed to parade his slides of family life before he began to twirl and spin his magic lantern.

We have been led into a trap. The close-printed, sun-lamped pages have been turned. We are snared. And can escape only by sharing, and surviving, the elemental mind-battles of the Recluse. Migraines mass like cumulo-nimbus armadas. There is nothing to divert our attention: no sub-plots, comic relief, or scholarly asides to mitigate against the rising shriek of horror. The poverty row cast features a faithful but brainless hound, Pepper, and a woman, Mary, who lurks in kitchens: sister or servant. She has no more substance than a Wyndham Lewis wife.

The story laid before us is the posthumous history of the Recluse's struggle; for his own soul, and for his conception of the cosmos that contains it. That struggle has been lost; it is all over—but it remains, as we follow its progress, an active concern. It comes to life in a perpetual, cyclic present. We are the mute audience who set the limits of this borderland, where the Recluse has pitched himself against "loneliness, silence, desert". He has perversely, conjured up this blasted and infertile place, the waste land, "shunned" and ill-reputed, as the setting for the grim sequence of events that he seems long ago to have anticipated, or even to have willed. The House has truly become the "synonym of all that was unholy and dreadful". The swine-things who rise from the pit to destroy him are of his own making: they are the breathing shape of his fear. He suffers in a series of accelerating visions, sweeping him far beyond the reach of all his conditioned reflexes, perhaps the most vividly realised and chilling "entropy tango" in fantastic literature.

And yet I persist in asserting that there is something coded and covert in this entire enterprise: some shadowy collaboration between author, editor, and journal-keeper. The Recluse has been gravity-chained to some ancient Faustian bargain that brings him back, time after time, to this House. Or to other versions of the House in other worlds. Even the violent geological shocks and spasms seem preordained. They do not surprise him. He is a post-traumatic man. He is almost incapable of wonder. His abiding humour is a clay and water sadness. He is the last of his tribe.

And why does the Recluse insist on depicting himself, rather like the young T. S. Eliot, with his congenital double hernia, as an elderly, damaged man—when he is later revealed, by the imperatives of the story, as "a great hale man who scarcely looked fifty . . . with coal black hair"? He is physically quite as powerful as the author, William Hope Hodgson, the Sandow-system body-builder who manacled Houdini with such savage fervour.

There are further and more sinister contradictions. The Recluse is no sportsman. He does not hunt, and yet he possesses a "rack of firearms" that would delight the most rabid Raccoon Mountain backwoodsman. Is he waiting, like Billy Bones, for the inevitable arrival of the black spot? It is, I fear, something far worse than that: a terror that has devoured all hope from his immortal soul.

The overgrown gardens, the cliffs, the tumbling falls rush from the catalogue of German Romanticism: the house is a conventional Expressionist set, to be admired but not lived in. It might have emerged from the radiation-sick dream of some paranoid seer, subjected by pioneer optimists to x-ray bombardments of the head. Its shape and character owe everything to the raked mind of a madman with a passion for symmetry. The thrust of the tower, containing the Recluse's study, is balanced by the uncharted spread of the cellars beneath. Dank zones of the psyche far better left unexplored.

"The cellars were really the most unlikely places in which to come across anything dangerous; considering that they can be entered, only through a heavy oaken door, the key of which, I carry always on my person." The Recluse might be defending himself against the unsubtle probings of a Jungian. The submerged mind, with its demons and ecstasies, remains a mystery that he is, stage by stage, and despite himself, drawn to explore. He was "curious, though in a frightened way, to know to what infernal place that hole led".

When he descends, most unwisely, into the pit, he carries a bundle of phallic toys: candles, double-barrelled shotgun, heavy horse-pistol. His conscience, the dog, is, for the moment, abandoned. The cellars connect with the pit in an undiagnosed chthonic system. The kingdom of the swine-creatures is near at hand. Only his demented physical energy repulses the communal stealth of the beasts. It is then that the material world fades, grows misty, is not to be trusted—and the Recluse "lifts" from this problematic zone to another dimension, where he is a watcher in a drama that takes him far beyond the circumscribed reach of his intelligence and his learning. "A quasi-Platonic world of ideas", as Brian Stableford describes it, "where the innate moral order of the cosmos is displayed in a series of physical representations and transactions" The hierarchy of ideas is demonstrated, made manifest, lived through. The shape of the transaction is clear: the Recluse, by risking the cellar and the pit, frees himself, in a natural reaction of contraries, to experience the Celestial Globes and the Green Star. By venturing out on the curvature of the unknown, he is re-turned to himself—enlightened, but diminished. He can no longer initiate the events that surround: he can only react.

But what is the derivation of these subterranean swine-creatures whose berserk raids keep the Recluse away from his study and his visions? There is a signal in the breezy confidence of Berreggnog's introduction to this landscape. He sketches, in the tones of the Anglo-Irish Ascendancy, his native "driver", as if he were putting the man forward for a cameo role in the novels of Somerville and Ross. "It's all in bed the lazy divvils is, sor". Could it be that the swine-creatures who break into the sunned house are avatars of the peasantry of the Gaelteacht, pre-mature Fenians? Creatures driven literally wild by hunger and poverty—until they are ready to hurl themselves against the obscene, half-deserted structures that represent their landlords and oppressors. These hairy-eared aboriginals, satirised by Myles na Gopaleen in *The Poor Mouth*, pigs with the "gift" of language, rise out of the smoky darkness to tear down the last redoubts of an alien "civilisation".

Now we must begin to unravel Hodgson's "inner-story". The narrative takes its tonal key from the poem, "Grief", which the editor found, "gummed in behind the fly-leaf of the MS." A tone of sentiment, loss, impotent regret: more Swinburne than swine-crazy. Some sickly guilt, "for that which *was*, and now is flown", lurks in the cellars like marsh-gas, swarms beneath the turbid waters of the pit. This secret sorrow implicates the Recluse's unconsummated love, floating out of reach, beyond the Sea of Sleep. Like all who keep private journals, he wants to confess. And, however much he circles the matter, he wants that confession to be understood.

The tale is almost told when we learn of the Recluse's arrival at the House on the Borderland, in the company of the woman, Mary, and "a large number of donkeys". The resonances are awkwardly familiar, blasphemous. He lets it be known, because that is what he wants to believe, that the woman is his "sister". Does this modest subterfuge, in fact, disguise the true reason for the flight into such a bleak exile? Were the couple pursued by the shadow of scandal, rumours of necromancy—or of incest?

I begin to convince myself that the nature of the taint that *ordains* the annihilation of every brick of this crumbling house is incestuous, feeding on itself; feverish, forbidden. Alan Aldridge's haunted skull was perhaps not so wide of the mark. The House becomes a Skull Castle, incubating guilt, turned desire, and the will towards self-destruction. It is as bleak, and weather-worn, as Elsinore, with its intestinal passages and haunted battlements. The Recluse's behaviour is abrupt, angular, perverse—unmotivated by the flow of the overt narrative. He treats his "sister" as if *she* were dangerous and mad. She was "like a frightened animal, and screamed aloud". "Could she be afraid of me? But no! Why would she?" The Recluse threatens "restraint". He carries her bodily to her room and locks her inside. "It was very queer she should have crept past my door . . . the thought occupied my mind, that it was not she, but some mystery of the house." Mary visibly shrinks from his touch. She goes so far, in his distress to struggle to unbolt the great door and let in the swine-creatures; to give them welcome . . . as the lesser evil.

Without doubt, Mary shares a forbidden secret: her experience of the love—that dare not speak its name. There is such a quirky, unbalanced construction when the Recluse recalls this period of transitory bliss. "Yes, though few knew it, none now save my sister Mary, I have loved and, ah! me—lost." Mary alone is involved in whatever has been abandoned. Can it be that she herself is the beloved one, a revenant cursing the house, held within its stout walls, and never to be "liberated" by the anarchic savagery of the pit-things? Mary is at the heart of the mystery; she is the source of the pain—an affair that was foresworn, botched, buried alive in the wilderness of Galway, beyond the pale of all liberal decencies. If this reading has any validity, then the whole mad setting begins to obey the rules of its own inverse logic.

Hodgson has successfully located his "greater story within the lesser". But how did he come by it, the "small book" with its "faint, pit-water smell"? Is it an accident that the discovery, by Tonnison and Berreggnog, was made in 1877, the year of Hodgson's birth. He used his secret knowledge to cross the "border of the Silences", to seize this overwhelming material, with its uncanny and dreamlike inevitability—but there was a terrible price. His withdrawal was made *from a premonition of his own death*. The bargain was struck. By some inspired act of occult mediumship he travelled ahead of himself. He entered his future as if it was a Book of the Dead. All the stages of his own extinction were made available to him. But the power was not to be lightly exploited. What followed was inevitable; now it was written.

On the outbreak of war in 1914, Hodgson returned from France to England. Overage, he insisted on joining up. During training, he was thrown from his horse: he was severely injured, and discharged. He recovered, re-enlisted; reached the Front by October, 1917. He died on 19 April, 1918, "blown to pieces" in a forward observation post. He was forty-one years old: not yet the age of the Recluse.

It comes in the end to this: a spread tarot of dark possibilities. A challenge to our sanity and our courage. The author parts from his creature. "The body under that coating, that shroud of dust, was neither more nor less than my own dead shell. I did not attempt to prove it. I knew it now, and wondered I had not known it all along. I was a bodyless thing." We are left holding an open book in our hand—in which the writer, posing as editor, sits in his study examining . . . an open book, in which a Recluse sits in his study, trying feverishly to fill the pages of his notebook, before the swine-creatures, whose feet he can hear on the stairs, padding along the corridor, *arrive.*

The pit has become a glassy lake across which William Hope Hodgson confronts the Recluse in a duel to the death. Both men write, faster and faster, to erase the shadow of their double; freeing themselves to enter the narrative they have, so far, only witnessed. If their concentration falters, they are lost. This precarious balance is maintained only with the complicity of a third party, a mute witness—the reader who seals the fatal triangle. And who dares not turn the book's final page, or walk away. The moment stretches until we can bear it no longer. The door is opening, "slowly", for ever. An intolerable movement that is destined never to be consummated.

Iain Sinclair
London, 1989

Acknowledgments

This edition of *The House on the Borderland* was published to commemorate the 100th anniversary of William Hope Hodgson's death, his life tragically cut short by artillery fire near Ypres, France in late April 1918.

To anyone who has ever felt, as I have, "infected by the novel's weird charisma"—this new edition is for you; I'd further like to extend my gratitude to those who channelled their cosmic contaminations into this project: John Coulthart, for his celestial vision and interior illuminations; David Kurzman, for generously allowing me to reprint Hodgson's signature from H. C. Koenig's copy of *The House on the Borderland*—the very copy read by Lovecraft, Derleth, and their circle of friends; Jon Mueller, for his soundtrack, rumbling and primal; Alan Moore, for his sensitive introduction, elevating Hodgson's achievement to its appropriate sphere; Iain Sinclair, for his grand wander from Borth to the Burren; and finally Meggan Kehrli, Ken Mackenzie, and Jim Rockhill, for sharing their talents and patience to produce this book.

The House on the Borderland was first published by Chapman and Hall in the spring of 1908. "An Aberrant Afterword: Blowing Dust in the House of Incest" was first published in the Grafton edition of *The House on the Borderland* in 1990. Alan Moore's introduction and John Coulthart's illustrations are original to this edition.